My life as a hashtag

D1531198

Gabrielle Williams

My life as a hashtag

ALLEN&UNWIN
SYDNEY · MELBOURNE · AUCKLAND · LONDON

THE WRITERS HOUSE

This project was assisted by a residency at Varuna the Writers' House

First published by Allen & Unwin in 2017

Allen & Unwin
83 Alexander Street
Crows Nest NSW 2065
Australia
Phone: (61 2) 8425 0100
Email: info@allenandunwin.com
Web: www.allenandunwin.com

A Cataloguing-in-Publication entry is available
from the National Library of Australia
www.trove.nla.gov.au

ISBN 978 1 76011 368 1

Teachers' notes available from www.allenandunwin.com

Cover and text design by Debra Billson
Cover images: hand girl © Wave/Stocksy; wolf-hat girl © Howl/Stocksy;
icons © inroad/Shutterstock
Set in 11.5/16 pt Adobe Garamond Pro by Midland Typesetters, Australia
Printed and bound in Australia by Griffin Press

10 9 8 7 6 5 4 3 2

The paper in this book is FSC® certified.
FSC® promotes environmentally responsible,
socially beneficial and economically viable
management of the world's forests.

To S&B with love

♡ ◯ ↱

18th September

These are what happy days looked like

Yumi's house was strictly back-door only.

The front door was for electricians, plumbers, and religious freaks rummaging in the shrubs for converts. It meant someone inside the house had to get up from what they were doing to let you in.

The back door required no more heavy lifting than an arm raised in a wave. The back door was friendlier. Which is why I always went through it.

Wilder was slouched on the couch, a movie streaming on the teev, his hand raised in a lazy wave as I came through the back door.

'Hey,' he said, without looking over at me.

'Hey,' I said back.

This is probably as good a time as any to tell you a little something about Wilder.

Wilder is Yumi's brother. If I were a couple of years older ... if I'd only just met Wilder at a party ... he'd be my number-one draft pick.

He has slim hips and long legs, and his fingers look like they belong on the keyboard of a piano.

His voice is deep and soothing. He should be on the radio. Except he's too handsome for the radio.

He has dark hair that he wears longish. Sometimes he tucks it back behind his ears, or pushes it off his face and keeps it there with one of Yumi's headbands.

His toffee-coloured eyes have a molten quality to them, like they've been poured straight from the saucepan. His mouth is slightly puffy, as if he's been punched, but you know he hasn't been punched because no one, no matter how crazy, would ever want to damage such a beautiful face. Sometimes he bites his bottom lip when he's thinking, creating a chink in the cushiony softness and breaking thousands of girls' hearts everywhere with that one tiny tooth-bite.

Wilder has this group of friends who are the same as him: a tsunami of cool and handsome, wrecking any female who happens to be in the vicinity.

Except me. They don't wreck me, because I've known them since they were toy-car-pushing, plastic-soldier-exploding boys. Since the days when the dining table would be draped with blankets and towels, and sandwiches would be slotted through to us by Yumi's mum as we sat cross-legged in the muddy light of the blanket-world.

I've been bench-pressed by Wilder – me and Yumi both have – when he hit thirteen and wanted to build up his muscles.

I've helped Yumi peel the skin off his back, when he got sunburnt a few summers ago.

I've spent as much time with Wilder as I have with my own brother. Wilder didn't wreck me. None of them wrecked me.

Actually, that's not strictly true. Harley ended up wrecking me. When he stopped talking to us all; stopped being friends with Wilder. But back when I was walking through Yumi's door that day ... back then ... Harley wasn't wrecking me yet.

Harley's my brother. One of the toy-soldier aficionados. Ever since we were kids, it'd been me and Yumi, Harley and Wilder.

Say goodbye to that.

But wait, this is supposed to be the happy part of the story. The sunshine, lollipops, rainbows and butterflies part.

This is the Before part.

'Where's Harley?' Wilder asked, his thumb scrolling upwards as he checked his news feed on his phone.

'He's coming,' I said.

The movie Wilder was watching had an old guy sitting behind a newscaster's desk, his hair wet like he'd been stuck in a downpour. There were a couple of clocks on the wall behind him showing different time zones. He seemed angry, going on about how banks were going bust, and people were scared of losing their jobs, and shopkeepers were keeping guns under their counters. Saying that the food was unfit to eat and the air was unfit to breathe; that things were bad – worse than bad; things were crazy, and we were all supposed to sit there and take it.

'What's this?' I asked, kneeling on an arm of the couch.

The same couch we'd dragged the cushions off all those years earlier to make teepee villages.

'*Network*,' he said. 'Number sixty-four.'

Wilder had started film school that year, and he'd made it his own personal mission to go through the Top One Hundred Movies of All Time. Anytime you went round there, he was as likely to be watching *The Babadook* (no. 71) as he was *Cool Hand Luke* (no. 67), or *Annie Hall* (62) or *Toy Story* (56).

Or *Network* (no. 64).

Yumi came in from the kitchen, a cheese toastie in her hand, her black hair pulled back into a messy ponytail.

'MC!' she said, putting her arm around me. 'I haven't seen you in ages.' (I'd seen her at school assembly ringing out the end of Term 3, Year 10 a couple of hours earlier). She smooched my cheek, then settled down on the arm of the couch next to me.

'Have you been watching this?' I asked her, my eyes fixed on the ranting man.

'A bit. But I got kind of bored. And toasted cheese sambos were calling me,' she added, looking with love and longing at the toastie between her fingers, then biting into it because she could resist no longer.

She was only human, after all.

'How can you say this is boring?' Wilder said to her. 'World's best – well, sixty-fourth best – movie of all time, classic Sidney Lumet, Academy Award winning, culturally significant, blah blah.'

'You're not even watching it,' Yumi pointed out to him. 'That's how amazing it is.'

Wilder chucked his phone onto the cushions of the couch and folded his arms across his chest, turning his face TV-side, to demonstrate watching-it for his sister.

Harley came in the back door and walked straight over to Yumi. 'Something smells good,' he said.

'That'd be me,' Wilder said.

'That's so sweet of you to make that for me,' Harley said, grabbing Yumi's arm and making like he was going to snatch the toastie out of her hand, his mouth open and ready to start chomping.

Yumi wrenched her toastie out of reach of his mouth. 'You know where the kitchen is, buddy boy.'

Harley let go of Yumi's arm and plonked himself down on the couch next to Wilder. 'What's this?' he asked, folding his arms across his body.

'*Network*,' I said. 'Number sixty-four. Academy Award Sydney Harbour something something.'

'Sidney Lumet,' Wilder said.

'Same difference.'

The newscaster guy was pointing his finger straight at the camera, saying that he was sick of us holding on to our toasters and our TVs and our steel-belted radials. He wanted us to get mad.

He stood up from his desk, agitated; waved his arms like an orchestra conductor motioning for all the instruments to play to the crescendo. He told everyone to stand up, to go to their windows ... to open them, stick their heads out, and yell, *I'm mad as hell, and I'm not going to take this anymore!* He windmilled his arms about, saying it over and over again, like he was stuck on a loop: 'I'm mad as hell, and I'm not going to take this anymore! I'm mad as hell, and I'm not going to take this anymore!'

The movie had our full attention now. It cut to a street scene, night-time, somewhere in New York. The weather was vicious, but people were opening their windows anyway, leaning out into the squalling rain, yelling that they were mad as hell, and they weren't going to take this anymore. A chorus of people, shrieking, howling, lightning spotlighting them and thunder underlining their fury.

I wanted to be there, in that moment, one of those shaggy-headed seventies girls living in New York, fire-escape stairs zigzagging across the back of my apartment building, yelling into the rain that I was mad as hell and I wasn't going to take it anymore.

I wasn't really. I wasn't mad as hell about anything – not back then I wasn't – but I couldn't remember the last time I'd yelled my loudest and stamped my foot. Probably not since I'd been a kid.

Wilder got up off the couch and walked over to the sliding doors leading out into the backyard. It was a beautiful start-of-spring day in Melbourne, sunshiny, clear blue, no clouds. A wash-load of clothes hung clipped to the clothesline outside; a Joy Division T-shirt pulled lazily against its pegs.

I knew exactly how warm the air would be when Wilder stepped into it, because I'd been walking in it only ten minutes earlier. It was the kind of temperature that is no temperature: where bare arms don't feel the lick of the sun or the bite of the wind, or even notice they're bare; the first warm day for months, where finally, finally, it feels like winter is packing up its bags and moving to the northern hemisphere to annoy the people there for a change.

Wilder stood on the back verandah for a moment, then he tilted his head up at the sky, threw his arms out crucifixion-style and howled, 'I'm mad as hell, and I'm not going to take this anymore!'

I could see, even from behind, that he was grinning. There was a flippantness to him; to the simple enjoyment of standing in the warmth and yelling abuse at no one in particular and everyone in general.

Harley laughed. He got off the couch and ran outside, doing a speccy on Wilder's back as he joined him, yelling that he was mad as hell too and wasn't going to take it anymore.

Yumi threw the crust of her nearly finished toastie onto the coffee table; then she grabbed my arm and ran me outside with her, yelling at the world before she'd even got past the couch, repeating the same sentence over and over, changing the way she said it, trying out a different emphasis on the words each time: 'I'm mad as *hell*, and I'm *not* going to take this anymore. *I'm* mad as hell, and I'm not going to *take* this any*more*.'

Standing with the three of them, I tilted my head upwards, facing the perfect blue of that early-spring day. I opened my mouth but, suddenly uncertain, my throat clamped like a vice, the words snagged on a vocal cord.

It felt strange, awkward. Like if I started yelling, someone would notice and yell back at me, 'You're not mad as hell. Not even by half.'

But then I realised that it was just noise. Freedom. Letting loose. No one would listen, and no one would care. The words unsnagged and came hurtling out of my throat, rattling against the trees in Yumi's backyard and blaring up into the cloudless blue of the sky.

'I'm mad as hell, and I'm not going to take this anymore. I'm mad as hell, and I'm not going to take this anymore. I'm mad as hell, and I'm *not* going to take this anymore.'

Putting the entire globe on notice – just because I could – that I was mad as hell.

And I wasn't going to take it anymore.

♡ ◯ ↷

Seven months later

16th April

The butterflies can't be trusted

Chapter 1

I sat on the train watching the wind rage at the tops of trees. Hassling, arguing, berating, tearing off leaves, throwing seed pods and branches onto the ground. Stomping its foot, having a tantrum.

Mad as hell at the world.

Welcome to autumn in Melbourne.

The clouds were dark and heavy, like they badly wanted to squeeze out even a baby-sized rainstorm, but the bambino was staying where it was, stubbornly refusing to be ejected from the cottonwool of the clouds. Maybe tomorrow the storm would come. Or later tonight at the party. Or maybe next week. Who knew.

I snapped a shot of my feet on the seat and sent it to Yumi, Liv, Anouk and Hattie.

'City. Lunch. Dad,' I captioned it.

It was a Saturday. And I'd brushed my hair.

I wouldn't normally have done either of these things:

brushed my hair, or gone into the city to meet Dad for lunch. But things were different now that Dad had moved out.

My parents had split up seven months ago. The day after Harley and I had been round at Yumi's place yelling that we were mad as hell.

Them splitting is no biggie in the scheme of things. Terrorists still blow up random public spaces. People off their heads on ice still attack whoever they've decided has looked at them funny. The globe is still warming like a pot of water on the stove.

A mum and a dad splitting up is microscopic. A speck on a speck of a speck. That's as much as it matters.

Except in our speck of a house, on our speck of a street, in our speck of a suburb, the split felt nuclear-bomb-ish. One atom's nucleus splitting into two unbalanced nuclei – me, Mum and Harley one fragment; Dad the other.

Explosions all round.

So now when I wanted to see Dad, I didn't go into the kitchen and shove him out of the way of the toaster, or take the remote from him and change the channel. Instead, I had to go round to Grandpa's house, where he was staying at the moment, or catch the train into the city to have lunch with him.

And on this particular day, in honour of lunch in the city, I'd brushed my hair.

I would generally consider myself to be a staunch anti-hair-brushing type of girl. I don't like how neat it looks when a brush has been dragged through it. Too fluffy. Too magnetised. Too to-the-shoulders.

When Dad lived at home, he'd look at me when I came downstairs and say, 'Your hair could do with a brush, MC. You look like the wreck of the *Hesperus*.' Whatever that was.

Actually, I can tell you; I googled it. After Dad moved out, I thought I should find out what he'd been saying to me all those years. I expected it would be something to do with Greek or Roman mythology – you know, like the Hydra or the Minotaur or Hercules – but it's not. It's a poem by this guy called Longfellow.

It's about the captain of a ship called the *Hesperus*, who takes his daughter on board for one of his trips. A crewman warns him that a hurricane is coming, that his daughter shouldn't come on the trip, but the captain ignores him, thinking he knows better. When the storm arrives, the captain lashes his daughter to the mast to prevent her from being swept overboard. The storm is so fierce that everyone on board dies, and the next morning a fisherman finds the daughter's body, still tied to the snapped-off mast, drifting in the surf.

A happy, cheery poem to refer to each morning when your daughter hasn't brushed her hair. Thanks, Dad.

So on this particular Saturday when I was catching the train into the city to have lunch with my dad, I brushed my hair.

Call it a peace offering, an olive branch. Call it an unwrecked *Hesperus*, daughter not yet lashed to the mast.

I got off the train at Flinders Street Station and walked up Elizabeth Street, the wind shoving me in the back, pushing at me, hurrying me along. The weekend-shopper crowds swirled around me, together with the autumn leaves. I slipped out of the mainstream and washed along Little Collins Street, away from Myer and David Jones and the Bourke Street Mall, towards my dad's work. Up the guts of the canyon created by the buildings. As I headed towards the mirrored, fuck-off towers of William Street, the wind still hassled me, like a drunk wanting my spare change, only leaving me alone once it had pushed me aggressively into the foyer of Dad's building.

I texted Dad. 'Downstairs.'

There was a gurgle of nerves in my stomach.

Nerves.

Over meeting my dad.

That's what happens when your folks split up. Suddenly, lunch with your dad feels like a date-type thing: a serious, important, don't-mess-this-up-type event, instead of a don't-brush-your-hair-because-who-cares-type meal.

I felt like things were fake-comfortable with Dad these days. Everything was nromal – you see what I did there? Exactly the same, but shifted around slightly.

He texted me back: 'Coming down.'

I stood by the lift and watched the numbers scroll up to the floor he worked on, then scroll back down from twenty-five through to seven, to six, five and four. I pushed my hair back behind my ears. It felt messy in my hand, so I checked myself in the mirrored door of the lift.

After all the effort I'd gone to brushing my hair, he wouldn't even know it.

Stupid autumn wind.

Stupid *Hesperus*.

Three. Two. One. The numbers of the lift changed to the letter 'G', the mirrored doors opened with a *ding*, and Dad came out smiling.

Behind him was a woman.

'You remember Tosca?' Dad said to me as he dragged me to him and gave my forehead a kiss. 'My PA?' he added.

He hadn't shaved.

He was wearing army fatigues, and a striped T-shirt.

He looked slightly crumpled.

I need to put this in perspective for you. Casual clothes were not a part of my dad's wardrobe vocabulary. He usually wore a suit and tie every day, or at very least a pair of smart pants and a polo top.

Army fatigues and a striped T-shirt? No.

Unshaved? No.

Crumpled? Definitely not.

He turned back to where Tosca was standing behind him and said to her, 'You remember my daughter, Marie-Claude? MC.'

I don't know why he threw the whole 'Marie-Claude' thing in there. No one ever calls me that.

Okay, Yumi and Liv occasionally call me 'Marie-Claude et Philippe, beep', because when they were learning French back in Year 7 they had to listen to *Les Aventures de Marie-Claude et Philippe* and recite the words in time, turning the page every time they hit a *beep*. Even now, four years down the track – neither of them studies French anymore – they still call me that sometimes.

But not Dad. Not until that particular day. *Tosca, meet Marie-Claude* (without the Philippe or the beep). It was just plain weird.

'Of course I remember Marie-Claude,' Tosca said. 'Hi.'

'MC,' I corrected her. 'I don't know why Dad just called me that. Why did you call me that?'

He hugged me to him again and kissed the top of my head. 'Don't know,' he said, then held me an arm's length away from him and looked at me. 'I thought maybe, because you're growing up – look how tall you're getting – maybe you needed a longer name to go with those long legs that you never used to have.'

I grinned at him.

I missed having him at home.

He should be home.

I looked at Tosca and smiled. I couldn't help feeling a bit sorry for her. Mainly because of her hair. Talk about wreck of the *Hesperus*. She obviously had no clue about Dad's preference for neatly brushed, slightly nerdy hair. Hers was an absolute mess, curls twisting out at all angles, defying gravity, defying science, defying maths, defying logic. It was like her hair was its own completely independent structure that just happened to be growing out of her head. It was the type of hair a person would never be able to have any control over. It wouldn't have mattered if she'd tied it up, straightened it out, wore a hat, or gelled it into a solid mass – it would still do whatever the hell it felt like. It was kind of great hair; the type of hair I loved. But I knew Dad would hate it.

'We've got this huge project going on at the moment,' Dad went on as he hugged me to him one last time then started walking towards the lobby doors, me and Tosca following, trying to keep up with his long, important strides, 'and Tosca's given up her weekend to help me, so I thought it only fair that she join us for lunch. That okay with you?'

'Yeah,' I said. 'For sure.'

Tosca had on a T-shirt with 'Harvard Law' written across it in big shouty letters, and 'just kidding' underneath in smaller letters. She was wearing bangles that clicked up her arm then clacked back down again whenever she moved it. She wore ripped jeans – Dad hated ripped jeans – and ankle boots – he wasn't crazy about those either, said they looked like something gnomes wore – and the softest leather jacket you'd ever seen, which even Dad couldn't not-like.

We walked back out into the wind, which jumped straight back onto me, tugging and pulling and behaving badly.

'What's with the beard, by the way?' I asked, my shoulder banging into him as the wind got particularly insistent. 'You look different.'

He grinned down at me. 'Well, you know what they say,' he said.

'What?'

'It's good for a man to have a hobby.' He laughed at his joke, and Tosca laughed too, the two of them grinning at each other.

The wind nudged me, taunted me, as if to say, *You're missing something.* As if Dad was obscuring something, performing a magician's trick, saying this thing over here with this mirrored hand – *Good for a man to have a hobby* – while the real meaning was smoking over in the hand I wasn't looking at.

When I got home from lunch in the city, Maude and Prue were sitting at the kitchen bench with Mum.

'… either way,' Maude was saying as I came in the back door, 'as soon as the money started rolling in, things changed.'

She put two fingers up towards Prue and then patted them against her lips, sign language for 'pass us a fag'.

They had used to go outside to smoke, the three of them. But since Dad had shifted out, all rules regarding ciggies and passive smoking – especially the damage it causes to young lungs, for example mine – had been skittled.

The three of them swivelled to look at me as I walked into the kitchen.

I went over to the fridge, opened it, looked inside for something to eat. Not because I was hungry, but because it's my stock-standard thing to do when I get home; a habit. I closed the fridge, went to the pantry, opened it. Nothing. Closed the pantry door and sighed, because there's never anything to eat in our house.

'How was lunch, darling?' Mum asked, tapping the tip of her cigarette against the lip of the ashtray then bringing it up to her mouth and dragging deep, as if it were a breath of fresh air.

Which, clearly, being a cigarette, it wasn't.

'Yeah,' I said. 'It was good.'

'How was Your Father?' she asked.

Your Father. With capital letters. Like she didn't really know him; hadn't been married to him for twenty years. Like he was My Father, and not related to her in any way.

I opened the drawer. Took out a glass. Went back to the pantry and took out the family-sized tin of Milo.

It was the only thing family-sized about us these days.

I could feel three sets of eyes on me as I walked over to the fridge.

'He was fine.' I shrugged.

I opened the fridge, took out the milk. Grabbed a spoon. Jemmied the lid off the Milo. Started scooping it into my glass.

I decided not to mention Tosca.

Well, I didn't not-mention her, but I didn't mention her, if you see the difference. Apart from anything else, it wasn't that big a deal. Not enough of a deal to mention.

'Where did you go after lunch?' Mum asked.

'What makes you think I went anywhere after lunch?'

'It's quite late,' she said, looking down at her watch.

'Oh. Right. Yeah. No, just lunch.'

I twisted the lid off the milk, admiring, as I did, my glossy, cool-as-fuck black nails that I'd had painted after lunch. It had been Tosca's idea to go and have a manicure. She'd gone for electric blue, and I'd chosen can't-go-wrong black.

I poured milk into my glass, the spoonfuls of Milo at the bottom too dense to be penetrated. Drinking Milo always reminded me of the outdoors – the dirt of the Milo and the sky of the milk.

I picked up my glass to take to my room. Which was when Maude slid her eyebrow up, just one, for emphasis, and said, 'I like your nails.'

Prue paused, her cigarette hand halfway to her mouth, and looked at my manicure. 'Very nice,' she agreed slowly, her chin dipping down towards her chest as she studied my hands.

I could feel the mood in the room mixing with the cigarette smoke to create a thickness, a slowing-down of time, but also the distinct fizzing, spitting sound – the crackle – of a fuse being lit.

The three of them looked at each other, then back at me.

'Where did you get those done?' Mum asked, taking my non-glass-holding hand in hers and examining my nails as if they were a clue.

'Um, South Melbourne?' I said. I could feel the booby trap in the conversation; I just wasn't sure where exactly it was and how exactly to step around it. 'We stopped on the way home. Dad took me to have a manicure.'

That was true. Ish. Dad *had* taken me to have a manicure. He was the one who had *paid* for my manicure. The fact that he hadn't actually sat in the next chair on from me, with his bangles jangling and his Harvard Law 'Just kidding' T-shirt on and his wrecked hair spiralling out of control – the fact that he wasn't the one getting his fingers and toes painted an electric blue – the fact that he wasn't the one asking what my favourite subjects were and which cute boys I liked – was beside the point.

The kitchen held its collective breath. One wrong move, and it was gonna go nuclear, I could tell.

'What a strange thing for Your Father to do,' Mum said.

'Very,' agreed Prue.

'Odd,' said Maude, scratching a match against the flint of the box and bringing the flame up to her ciggie.

'Dad took you to have a manicure?' Mum checked, tilting her head to the side, as if that angle would help her see past any distractions. 'This afternoon? After you had lunch?'

'Yeah.'

Tick. Tick. Tick.

'Just you and Your Father?' Maude asked. I could smell sulphur as she blew out the match – a devilish, dangerous odour in my nostrils.

Tick. Tick. Tick.

Sitting in the massage chair as my nails had been painted earlier, a thought had bubbled into my head: that it was strange Tosca was still hanging out with Dad and me, even after we'd had lunch.

When Dad had offered to drive her home, and then took me first, the bulbous thought had dropped down into my throat, making a glutinous lump.

When I'd got out of the car and Tosca had said to me, 'Thanks for letting me crash your lunch. Might see you again sometime soon,' the lumpish thought had slipped from my throat and wedged itself in my chest.

But it was only now, standing in the kitchen with Mum and Maude and Prue looking at me, that the wedged thought detonated in my chest into fully fledged knowledge.

Dad had brought Tosca along because he wanted me to meet his new girlfriend.

It was so obvious, I could feel my cheeks burn with the humiliation of not having picked up on it till this moment.

And now it was up to me to tell Mum about her.

Thanks, Dad.

Mum leant forward on her elbows, her eyes watching me carefully. She knew. She knew, without me having to say it, that there had been someone else at lunch with us.

Maude dragged on her fag, blowing the smoke out in a long, slow bloom. She knew too. She and Prue and Mum all knew.

The kitchen was poised.

There were no cooking smells. Nothing simmering away in a saucepan on the cooktop. No frying onion smells. No spaghetti bolognaise smells. Mum didn't cook anymore, not like she'd used to. Without Dad around, she couldn't be bothered with the chopping and the shopping and the preparing and the organising and the stirring and the saucepans and the pots and the wooden spoons that went into making a home-cooked meal.

We were eating a lot of takeaway.

And smoking inside plenty.

'MC?' Mum pressed. 'Just you and Dad?'

24

There are photos of my mum from when she was my age, her hair blonde, her face open. Making rabbit ears behind people's heads; laughing with a random boy; standing on one leg with her arms spread out away from her body; cramming into an old-fashioned phone booth with a bunch of other people; staring into the camera, with heart-shaped sunglasses on her face. She looks like exactly the sort of person I would be friends with.

And now here she was, forty-something, sitting in our kitchen, a spiral of smoke rising from the fag between her fingers, about to hear the news that I'd just gone for a manicure with probably the last person in the world she wanted me to hang out with.

I looked down at my treacherous nails, each one propped on the end of each finger like an accusation. Like an admission.

Pointing the finger had never seemed so literal.

I took a sip of my Milo, watching the three of them over the rim of my glass. And then I brought my drink down away from my face and said, 'Well, um, you know Tosca?' and braced myself for the explosion.

I felt myself flinch, waiting for it.

But instead, there was nothing.

Silence.

A void.

It made me wonder whether I had it wrong. Maybe my nails weren't being treacherous. Maybe it was just a manicure after all. Innocent. No big deal.

Mum took a deep breath. She tilted her head back and looked up at the ceiling, dragged deep on her ciggie, then dropped her chin back to look at me and blew out a plume of smoke.

'Who's Tosca?' Prue and Maude said at the same time.

'Tosca,' Mum said, with something resembling satisfaction – but it wasn't satisfaction; it was like the toxic cousin of satisfaction – 'is Dennis's PA.'

Maude shook her head, *tsk*-ing with her tongue.

'Oh, for God's sake,' Prue said, tipping a new ciggie out of the pack and lighting it. 'That man is the biggest cliché there is. No offence, but seriously. His PA? And let me guess – she's younger than him.'

I wanted to take it back. *No, not Tosca. Someone else. No one you know. Just some person. Not Tosca. Just me and Dad. The two of us, lunch for two, him and me, that's all, la-di-da.*

'Tosca,' Mum said again, shaking her head.

I gripped my Milo and realised, as I looked at the three of them sitting at our kitchen bench, that this was how it was going to be from now on. Instead of Mum and Dad, it was going to be Mum *or* Dad. A choice constantly having to be made. A seesawing negotiation that I would never be able to win. A right and a wrong answer, reversed depending on who you were with.

I thought back to when I was little and Dad would come home from work. I'd hear his key in the door, and I'd run down the hallway, scoot up into his arms, and tell him what I'd done at kinder – the sandpits I'd played in, the climbing frames I'd climbed over – so happy to have him home.

But then I'd got older and lazier, and when he'd come home I'd be kind of busy, watching telly or doing homework or scrolling through Insta, and I'd look up from whatever screen I was on, and he'd kiss me on the cheek or the top of my head and say, 'How's your day been?' and I'd say, 'Alright,' and that was it.

And now I couldn't take that back; couldn't change how I'd been when he'd walked in the door. But the thing was – the unfair thing was – I hadn't known there was a possibility that he would stop coming home. If he'd warned me, if he'd said to me, 'This might stop – this, me, here, coming home each night – it might not keep going,' then I'd have gone back to running down the hallway and making a big deal of him when he'd got in from work.

I hadn't known.

I should have known, but I hadn't. I needed everything spelt out for me.

Including the fact that Tosca was Dad's girlfriend.

Chapter 2

After Mum and Prue and Maude had grilled me in the kitchen (the most cooking Mum had done since Dad had moved out) I went upstairs and lay on my bed with my pillow hugged to my stomach, the glass of Milo sitting ignored on my bedside table.

Dad had a girlfriend. Her name was Tosca.

Every morning, for the entire time that he'd lived at home, he'd complained that my hair was unbrushed, and now he had a girlfriend – strange word, when used in the same sentence as 'my dad' – whose hair messed all over mine.

I'd even brushed my hair to go and meet him. Hah. Sucked in, me. I was glad the wind had wrecked it. Glad he hadn't seen that I'd dragged a brush through my hair especially for him.

I almost felt angry with him. Except he was my dad, and I hardly got to see him anymore – I didn't want to spend the time I had with him feeling angry.

I heard the door to my bedroom bang open.

'Who died downstairs?' a voice said, then a body threw itself onto the bed at my feet.

Liv.

Liv lives next door.

Try saying that three times fast.

I looked down the length of the bed at her. 'What about downstairs?'

'The three of them in the kitchen, looking so serious.' Liv pushed the sleeves of her jumper up to her elbows, then changed her mind and pulled the whole thing over her head and dumped it on the floor. 'Mum looks like she's about to stage an intervention or something.'

Liv's mum is Prue – the one who was down there with Mum and Maude, smoking and fagging and grilling me about Dad's new girlfriend.

I lifted my legs up so that my feet faced the ceiling, toes nearly touching the hanging mobile that I was far too old for, its flowers naive and innocent-looking, from a time when I'd been the same. Dad had put it up for me when we'd first moved into this house. I'd been meaning to take it down for years, but now that he'd moved out it would seem like bad luck to remove it.

I flopped my feet back down onto the bed. I wanted to tell Liv that I'd had a shitty day. That Dad had a girlfriend, that Mum was pissed off, and that I was the one who'd had to tell her.

'Nice top,' I said instead.

Liv looked down at her chest as if she didn't remember what she was wearing, then nodded at me, completely and utterly unconcerned.

'Oh yeah. Yours. I came in and grabbed it while you were out. I got this skirt this morning from the op shop' – she pinched at the tartan pleated skirt, which looked like something out of Scotland in the seventeen hundreds – 'and thought your top would go perfectly.'

'That's the ugliest skirt I've ever seen,' I said. 'Seriously.'

'Why spank you,' she said, then gathered it up on one side and tied it into a knot at her thigh so that all the pleats concertinaed like a half-open accordion. 'What do you think?' she asked, looking down at the knotted pleats.

'Worse.'

'Well, spank you two times.' She grinned.

I sighed.

'The top's BOY, though,' I added.

BOY. Better on You. A little something my friends and I made up. My clothes are always BOY. Or more specifically, BOL: Better on Liv. Liv doesn't seem to care about what she's wearing, what she looks like, whether something fits or not. She can probably afford to be like that because everything looks Better on Liv. She's like a coathanger, angular and wiry, with cropped hair and eyes that look directly at you, pierce you, then crinkle up in a naughty smile.

Which was how she managed to get away with wearing a tartan skirt that was long and misshapen and circa Battle of Hastings. And my T-shirt.

She pulled my shirt out from her stomach to look upside-down at the print of Bambi on the front of it. 'Maybe I should keep it,' she said, patting Bambi possessively back against her body. 'Seeing as it looks so good on me.'

'Huh,' I grunted, then shifted so that I was sitting up cross-legged, leaning against my bedhead.

'Dad's got a girlfriend,' I said, holding up my nails as if that explained everything. 'We went and got a manicure together today. Which is kind of weird now that I say it like that, but I didn't realise she was his girlfriend at the time.'

Liv kneeled up and stuck flat one of the magazine pages on my wall that had folded up at the corner.

'When did you figure out she was his girlfriend?' she asked.

I sighed. 'When your mum and Maude and my mum made a big deal about my nails.'

Liv raised her eyebrows. 'Nails don't mean she's his girlfriend.'

'I know, but … I don't know. I think they're right. I think she is.'

'What's her name?' Liv asked, dragging my laptop up off the floor, pulling it onto her lap and flipping it open. Typing in my password.

'Tosca,' I said. 'She's Dad's PA.'

I looked over Liv's shoulder as she logged into my Facebook account, went to Dad's profile; scrolled down.

It was strange. I'd never thought to have a look at Dad's Facebook. It turned out he had two hundred and seventy-three friends, which is probably not bad for an old guy.

I guess. I mean, who knows. Liv scrolled down through all the familiar and unfamiliar faces Dad was friends with.

And then we saw her. Tosca. With her hair looping in crazy corkscrews, and her eyes crinkled in a smile, looking up at whoever was taking the photo.

'Is that her?' Liv asked.

I nodded.

'What's she like?'

'Well, she's nice, I guess,' I said. Liv clicked on Tosca's profile, and we went through her photos: parties she'd been at, in dark rooms with twinkly lights and crowds of people, her arms around girlfriends, grinning at the camera. 'At least, that's what I thought until I found out she was shtupping my dad. Now I'm not sure what I think of her.'

The photos on Tosca's page could have been of me and Liv and Yumi and Anouk and everyone.

She could have been a friend of mine. Could have been at any one of our parties.

She could have been someone I'd hang out with. If I was, like, twenty-four or something, and not sixteen.

'But, it's kind of pretty bad,' I went on, not sure how much to say, how to express it, 'because, you know, Mum, it's pretty bad for her. She's pretty cut up.'

Mum's face had changed in that moment when I'd said Tosca's name. It had literally seemed to harden around her mouth and her eyes, as if she'd never truly laugh again.

Liv kept scrolling down through Tosca's friends. 'She looks young,' she finally said.

'Yeah, she's, I don't know, twenty-something. Maybe?'

Liv whistled. 'Score: your dad, I guess.'

I didn't answer. Yes, of course it was a score for Dad. Tosca was young and gorgeous and looked like exactly the sort of person you'd want to be friends with. Tosca was a game-changer.

Score indeed.

And then we saw, slotted in among all her other photos, a shot of Tosca and my dad. They were laughing at something, coats on, collars up, his arm resting along the back of her chair, a perfect, matching pair.

Something about the photo seemed familiar. I looked closer.

It had been taken at Grandpa's house, in the backyard, the wisteria above their heads leafless and bony, like a skeleton grasping at the pergola.

The wisteria at Grandpa's had gone through its whole big-purple-pendant-flowers phase and was now at the shedding-leaves stage; it definitely wasn't skeletal. It hadn't been skeletal since last winter.

The photo of Dad and Tosca had been taken deep in winter. Last year.

At Grandpa's.

Back before Dad had moved out.

I felt my eyes sting. Somehow, that made everything so much worse. Like Grandpa had been in on it. Like it was definite that there were two sides now, Dad's side and Mum's side, and Grandpa was staunchly on Dad's side.

I wanted to be on both sides. I didn't want to have to choose.

I leant back against my pillows and looked up at the ceiling. The flowers of my mobile dangled limply, like they needed water. Like they could barely be bothered hanging from the hook.

I stood up on my bed and unhooked it.

It seemed stupid to hold on to old memories when a few streets away, Dad was busy making new ones.

\#

Liv was still wearing my Bambi T-shirt and her op-shop tartan skirt knotted at the thigh when we got round to Yumi's place later that arvo.

There was a party on at Jed's that night, and a few of us were going to get ready over at Yumi's.

Jed's.

Jed's.

And once more for good luck.

Jed's.

Jed has these blue, blue eyes and cheeks that look like someone's slapped him over his bad behaviour. Because he's bad. That's for sure.

It's one of the things I like about him.

Liked.

He has this party trick that always gets a reaction. If he's over at someone's house and he sees that they've got a fishbowl, he always checks out the fridge to see if there's a carrot in there. Then he grabs a knife and slices a length of carrot – you hardly even notice he's doing it; he's chatting away while he's slicing – and he puts the rest of the carrot back in the fridge, and you keep on talking. A bit later, when he finds himself next to the fishbowl, he starts talking about the fish, saying how pretty they are, how much he loves fish, how much he really, really loves fish, how fish are one of his favourite things … and then he plunges his hand into the bowl, water splashing out onto the floor, and he pulls out a sliver of orange – the carrot he cut earlier in the night. He holds it up above his mouth for a second, making it wriggle like it's alive, and then he drops it into his mouth, crunching down on it, freaking out anyone who's standing close.

Not me, because I've seen him do it a few times; I'm used to it. But if you're not used to it, you're guaranteed to think he's just taken a goldfish out of the bowl and chowed down on it. The crunch of the carrot makes it especially convincing.

It's pretty funny. In a very bad way.

So yeah, Jed.

A couple of weeks earlier, Jed had posted a video of his dog, the Gun, on Facebook. The Gun's mouth was moving exactly like a human being's, and he was saying, 'The olds aren't in Melbourne on the sixteenth, so Jed and I thought some of you bee-atches – that's a female dog, so it's totally legit for me to say that – might want to come round and sniff some butt. What? That's what dogs do for good times. BYO humans. Party in the doghouse!'

The last couple of times I'd seen Jed at parties, he'd made some pretty serious moves on me. But I figured there was no way I could ever kiss him, because there were complications.

Anouk-sized complications.

A quick explanation – something you'll need for later on: over summer, Anouk had been up at Merimbula with her folks, and Jed had been up at Merimbula with his folks, and they'd hooked up a couple of times. Nothing had happened between them since they'd come back to Melbourne, but Anouk had put the word out that she liked him. She'd written his name all over her schoolbooks; she'd love-hearted his initials on her iPad cover. So he was now pretty much off limits to all of us – to any of Anouk's friends.

Because, you know, sisters before misters.

The last time I'd seen Jed was at a party at Emile's. It was late in the night and Jed had his arm resting on the wall above my head. He'd looked into my eyes and stepped in closer, so he was only a pout away.

I had thought my chest might explode all over him.

Which would have made things awkward.

And then Hattie had come and dragged me by the arm over to everyone else because she was having a Snapchat emergency – 'And if you're not in the pics, it's like you weren't even here, and so, yeah, I need you over here' – and while she was all Snapchat emergency-ing, I knew that the real reason she'd dragged me away was as a warning to step away from the cute guy.

To let me know that Anouk wasn't happy.

So, I'd stepped away. Because who wanted to be the person to kiss the guy Anouk liked and then have to deal with the fallout the next day? Bags not.

Hattie and Anouk are super-tight.

Me, Liv and Yumi are super-tight.

Other girls in our group are super-tight.

And like a Venn diagram, all our super-tight smaller groups overlap into one gigantic group of solidarity and general party good times and, like I said before, sisters before misters.

So, on that particular night, we were going over to sniff some butts at Jed's (just saying, that's specifically what the Gun invited us over for), but I wouldn't be able to kiss Jed even if he wanted to kiss me, because Anouk still had first dibs on him. Even all these months on from Merimbula.

Liv and I walked in the back door at Yumi's. Wilder was slouched on the couch, watching something on TV – as usual. He held his hand up in a lazy wave – as usual. But things were vaguely off-kilter with Wilder these days. He was still the same towards me, I was still the same towards him, but there was a Harley-shaped hole in the room now, and I didn't know why. All I knew was that Harley and Wilder weren't hanging out anymore.

Seventeen years of friendship – since they were kids together at kinder – gone. Like it hadn't even mattered.

I'd asked Harley a few times what was the matter, but he'd acted like he didn't know what I was talking about; said he was busy, that uni was full-on, that everything was cool between him and Wilder, he was just doing other stuff and didn't have time to go round there anymore.

The most words I seemed to get out of Harley these days were *it's fine, nothing, you don't know what you're talking about*, and that was on a good day – mostly he'd just stalk off to his bedroom or out of the house without replying to me, a pissed-off tilt to his shoulders.

I'd thought of asking Wilder what the problem was – what had gone wrong – but Yumi had already tried, and he'd reacted the same way that Harley had – nothing had happened, everything was fine – and if that was what he was telling his own sister, it was a fairly safe bet that he'd tell me the same thing.

So I didn't ask.

Liv and I went and stood behind the couch to see what Wilder was watching. There was a brawl going on in a riverside bar, fairy lights reflected in the water. Some chick smashed a guitar over someone else's head. People were being thrown in the river. Men were corkscrewing down to the ground after being punched; women had their hands up to their faces in horror. A band played on a podium, and as the fighting became more hectic the conductor got the musicians to change the tempo to something a little more pacy to match the action on the dancefloor.

Clearly it was a comedy. I'm not saying it was funny. I'm just saying it was meant to be.

'What's this?' I asked, leaning forward over the back of the couch.

'*Roman Holiday*,' Wilder said.

Liv climbed over the back of the couch and sat down beside him. I went and sat down on the couch arm next to Liv.

'What number?' Liv asked.

'Fifty-seven.'

Audrey Hepburn was the chick with the guitar, smashing the guy on the head; I recognised her now. It looked like there were these dark, spy-type guys trying to kidnap her, and these other two guys trying to stop her from being kidnapped.

I texted Yumi. 'On couch. Come down.'

Audrey Hepburn and this dark-haired dude were running along the river, but one of the spy-guys was around the corner, waiting for them. He punched the dark-haired guy in the face – 'in the kisser' is, I'm certain, what would have been written in the script; it was the fifties, after all. The spy-guy tried to grab Audrey Hepburn but she punched him, and before he could do anything more, she jumped into the river with the dark-haired dude and they swam away.

Yumi came downstairs in her trackpants and a holey T-shirt. She sat on the floor on front of Wilder and Liv, leaning back against the couch. Looking at her profile, with Wilder's profile behind her, I was struck by how like Wilder Yumi was – a girl version. She was finer, smaller, but she had the same dark hair, same amber eyes, same tsunami coolness. The only difference was the girlness of her, and the smudged freckle under her eye resembling a tear, which always made her look slightly sad, even when she was laughing her head off.

'What's this?' she asked.

'*Roman Holiday*,' Liv said.

'Fifty-seven,' I added.

Anouk came in the back door, looking down at her phone, a wolf hat jammed on the top of her head.

'Nice hat,' Liv said.

'Why, spanks,' Anouk said, glancing up from under the brim of the wolf's toothy jaws, her big doe-eyes looking unworried by the fact that a gigantic wolf had her entire head engulfed in his mouth.

'You remind me of someone,' Liv said, frowning.

Anouk raised an eyebrow, knowing that whatever was going to come next was going to be sarcastic.

'Hang on a minute,' Liv went on, clicking her fingers as if she were trying to conjure the name out of the air in front of her, 'hold on a sec, I've nearly got it. It's … it's … hang on, it's coming … I know! It's Little Red Riding Hood. Post-eating.'

'Excusay moi,' Anouk said, 'but if you knew anything, you'd know Little Red Riding Hood wasn't actually eaten by the wolf – the grandma was. So if I look like anyone, it's a half-chewed granny.'

Liv laughed.

'Watching a movie here,' Wilder said. 'Trying to.'

Anouk sat on my knee and gave me a kiss on the cheek. 'Thank God you're here,' she said to me, then she glanced over at Liv. 'Remind me why I hang out with you?'

'Because I'm irresistible,' Liv said, cocking a shoulder and putting on her version of Irresistible Face.

'And because, through her, you get to hang out with me,' Yumi added from her spot on the floor.

'True,' Anouk said, wriggling into position on the couch between Liv and me, her arm still slung over my shoulder. 'All excellent reasons.'

Hattie came in the back door, still in her basketball gear, her face still flushed. 'Omigod, I'm so wrecked,' she said, plonking herself down on the ground next to Yumi. 'I'm not even sure I can be bothered going tonight.'

Of course she was going tonight; as if she wasn't going tonight.

'You should have seen the other team, they were psycho bitches. Look at this scratch one of them gave me.' She held her arm out so everyone could admire the long red divot down the inside of her wrist. 'I felt like saying to them, *Hello, it's just a game, no one's going to die if the ball doesn't go in the basket.* Although of course because they were such heinous bitches, there was no way we were going to let them win. So that was satisfying. What's this, anyway?'

'Gregory Peck,' Wilder said, nodding towards the dark-haired guy on the screen, 'is a news reporter, but Audrey Hepburn doesn't know it. She's a princess who's run away because she's sick of being a princess. They met by accident, he realised she's a big story, that he can make five grand out of her, so he's spent the day taking her around Rome while his mate has been taking secret photos of her. But now some government agents have found her and are trying to take her back to the palace.'

Audrey and Gregory sat shivering under a bridge in their wet clothes. Gregory put his arm around Audrey to keep her warm. And then they looked at each other, the music swelled (like music always does in old movies), and they kissed.

'So he's just in it for the money?' Liv checked. 'The news story? Is that right?'

'Yeah.'

'But he's kissing her anyway.'

'Yeah.'

'Bastard.'

Spoiler alert. In the end, Gregory Peck decides not to write the story, not to collect five thousand dollars, not to pass Go, because he's fallen in love with Audrey, and she's fallen in love with him. But they can't be together because she's a princess, and he's not a prince.

Apparently these sorts of things were very strict in the fifties. You love him? You're one of the most powerful women in the kingdom? Sorry, you still can't marry him, because he's not a prince.

By this stage, all us girls were crying on the couch and floor. Well, not Liv of course, because she's a hard-arse, but the rest of us were face-wet-with-tears sobbing.

Wilder looked at us and grinned. 'Omigod,' he said, 'I didn't realise you girls were such romantics.'

'I can't believe you're not crying,' Hattie said. 'Is your heart made of stone? Is there actually a real live person in there, or are you some kind of robot with a battery where your heart should be?'

Wilder doesn't wreck me. I told you that already. But he definitely wrecks Hattie. She always saves a little glitter in her eyes for when she looks at him.

Wilder grinned back at her and punched his own chest a couple of times, like, *Nothing to see here.*

'I'm not crying,' I said. 'I've got something in my eye, that's all.'

'I'm thinking about an assignment I've just remembered is due on Monday,' Yumi said.

And then Anouk said, 'I'm crying because Gregory Peck looks exactly like Jed.'

I felt annoyance spark in my chest. Jed and Gregory Peck looked nothing alike.

She'd only said that to make sure everyone remembered Jed was off limits. That them there were the rules. That it was hands off her guy.

That the only person allowed to kiss Jed tonight was her.

#

Yumi's bedroom has multiple sports medals hooked over the arms of multiple championship cups, which jostle for room on her bookshelves and desk with multiple excellence awards and coach's awards. Netball, footy, running, tennis – Yumi is most excellent at all of them.

Her walls are plastered with vintage posters from bands her mum went and saw when she was our age or a bit older:

an orange Elvis Costello poster with 'Get Happy' written across it in sky-blue writing; a Smiths poster featuring a photo of Elvis Presley (who clearly didn't play with the Smiths, but whatever); another Smiths poster with 'Girlfriend in a Coma' written across the top. Bronski Beat. Siouxsie and the Banshees. Duran Duran.

A couple of years back, Yumi found a dusty turntable and a box of records at a garage sale, so afternoons spent at her place usually consist of the crackling, needle-in-the-groove sound of John Lennon's *Imagine*, Stevie Wonder's 'Wonderland', *This is Hip* by John Lee Hooker, that type of thing. An audio pairing to the posters on her walls.

The night of Jed's party, Liv, Hattie, Anouk and I were putting on our make-up, Yumi was in the shower, and the Mamas & the Papas were on the turntable – *16 of Their Greatest Hits*, if you don't mind.

Ancient school.

The cover of the album had the four members of the band standing in a park looking straight at the camera, a willow tree behind them; two guys, two girls. The two guys and one of the girls looked appropriately hippy, but then standing in the middle of the group was one bad-arse mofo with her hands on her hips, looking like she'd smack your face if you said even slightly the wrong thing.

'She choked on a sandwich, you know,' Liv said, taking the album cover out of my hands and pointing at the bad-arse mofo. 'Mama Cass did.'

Anouk raised one eyebrow. 'No, she didn't,' she said.

'Yeah,' Liv said. 'She did.'

Anouk picked up her phone and tapped at the screen. 'Cass Elliot,' she started reading, scrolling through various links. 'Mamas & the Papas. Blah blah. Rock & Roll Hall of Fame. Yada yada. Death. Collapsed on *The Tonight Show* with Johnny Carson. No, hang on, that's not it. Here you go: "An oft-repeated urban legend"' – and here she raised both eyebrows at Liv – '"claims that Elliot choked to death on a ham sandwich … a partially eaten sandwich found in her room might have been to blame … post-mortem showed she died of a heart attack and no food was found in her windpipe". I think you'll find that's what's called an urban legend.' Her mouth stretched over the words as she ostentatiously pronounced 'urban' and then 'legend'.

'Consider yourself schooled by Google,' Hattie said, leaning in to the mirror and putting mascara on.

Yumi came back from her shower, stepping over those of us who were sitting on the floor so she could get to her wardrobe and get out some clothes. 'No, don't anyone move, I'm fine with stepping over all of you. Seriously, don't even move your legs a little bit, I'm fine,' she said.

Because, yeah, she needed us to move our legs.

I shifted out of Yumi's way and took the album cover back from Liv. 'I love the fact that her top has creases across the lap from where she was sitting,' I said, pointing at Mama Cass, 'like it hadn't occurred to her for even one second to maybe grab an iron before the shot was taken for the cover of their album.'

'I hardly think you can talk,' Liv said, pulling at my unironed Bambi T-shirt. 'Don't think you did a whole lot of ironing of this little baby.'

I laughed. 'Well, that's only because I didn't realise you were going to be breaking into my house this morning, stealing my T-shirt, and wearing it to the party tonight. If I'd known, I definitely would have ironed it for you first.'

'Is that yours?' Anouk said, flicking her eyes over at the Bambi top, then looking back at me. 'It's cute as.'

'Yeah,' I said.

'You should be wearing that tonight,' she said. Emphasis on 'that'. 'It'd look so good' – emphasis on 'so' – 'with that skirt you're wearing.'

It sounded nice, all sugar and spice ('that would look so good on you') – but what she was really saying ('what you've got on now doesn't look as cracking as that other top') was all slugs and snails.

Anouk is gorgeous and smart, and she's excellent fun to be around. She writes Shakespearean sonnets that are funny and cool, riffing on why soy milk shouldn't be allowed in the same room as coffee, or the fact that meerkats require a name change because they're not actually cats. But she's tricky, too, because she always does this kind of thing with me – the slugs and snails thing – though I'm never completely sure if she does it deliberately or if I'm just being over-sensitive.

I looked at myself in the mirror; at the old Radiohead T-shirt I was wearing with my short denim skirt. The Bambi T-shirt definitely would have looked better.

'What the fook, Anouk,' Liv said. 'She can't wear this because, hello, I'm wearing it. And I'm not giving it book.' Twisting the word 'back' so that it rhymed with fook. And Anouk.

Anouk laughed.

That whole 'fook Anouk' thing? It was a running joke that had been going on between us for a good couple of years now, ever since Anouk was first called Anouk by an emergency teacher back in Year 9.

Her real name is Annick.

The emergency teacher – who was quite handsome, incidentally – was doing the rollcall, and when he came to Annick, he said, 'Anouk?'

Anouk said, 'it's Annick actually, not Anouk,' as if it mattered (which it didn't, because he was only going to be taking us for a week).

That was when Liv leant over and said, quietly – not so the emergency teacher would hear, but so the rest of us could – 'Annick, Anouk, who gives a fook,' and we all collapsed into giggles.

The poor guy never ended up getting us under control. He probably gave up teaching as a vocation once he'd had us for the week, because for the rest of his time with us, every class, he had to contend with an endless round of hands going up to answer questions using words that rhymed with Anouk.

Book was used a lot. Duh.

Hook.

Look.

Crook, nook, rook, sook, shook, took. They were all fair game. One time Anouk even managed to throw in Innsbruck, which was quite an achievement.

And ever since then, Annick has been called Anouk.

#

Anouk sat opposite me on the tram to Jed's party, going through her phone, the rolling amble of public transport making her and Hattie sway like they were underwater mermaids. Or in Anouk's case, an underwater mermaid with a wolf chowing down on her.

I took a photo of the two of them leaning in towards each other like they were magnetised, Anouk holding her fingers up at me in a peace sign, the rest of her hand still clutched around her phone, Hattie with a matching peace sign and her tongue poking out.

Then I snapped a selfie of me and Liv and Yumi.

All in the name of Snapchat.

We were talking French. All of us. Not that any of us particularly spoke French (though Liv and Yumi did remember a few words from back in Year 7 and 8), but we'd decided before we'd got on the tram that we'd speak French for the entire trip.

'*Mon dieu elevasion*,' Anouk said.

'Haw haw haw, *mélange, a toi*,' Yumi threw back.

None of it actually meant anything. Well, some of the words did, but most of them were French-ish sounds, delivered with the thickness in the throat and the roll of the tongue that we thought made us sound particularly authentic.

We threw in '*oui*' (yes), '*bonjour*' (hello), '*Marie-Claude et Philippe beep*', '*croissant d'orange*' (orange croissant), '*quelle heure et il?*' (what hour is it?) and '*la petite fleur comment allez vous*' (little flower how are you), giggling as we ran out of words we knew and started throwing in whatever we thought sounded French, getting louder and louder, talking over each other, competing to see who could sound the most Gallic.

And Anouk looked over at me, laughing, and said ... well, I couldn't be sure, everyone was talking, throwing in stupid-sounding French, but it sounded like she said, '*Le garçon.*' Then she winked at me, and pursed her mouth into a kiss.

Le garçon. The boy.

Jed.

Consider yourself officially warned, she might as well have said to me.

Officially warned in French.

Chapter 3

It was late in the night.

Jed and I were sitting by the pool, on banana lounges.

Jed and me.

Oh yeah.

Actually, it was Jed and me and the Gun. His dog – the one who'd invited us – was sitting up, his back straight, his ears pitched forward, watching all the people partying at his house.

'He doesn't seem all that happy to have us here,' I said to Jed, raising my eyebrows in the Gun's direction. 'I mean, hello, you invite a whole lot of people over,' I said to the Gun, 'you've got to expect them to come. Maybe some drinks will spill. Maybe some cigarettes will be smoked. It's just the way of the party, and you can't worry your doggy head about it.'

Jed laughed.

The wind from earlier in the day had slunk off, ashamed of its bad behaviour, leaving the night warm and slightly static. A storm still waited in the clouds, but it didn't have the va-voom necessary to let rip yet. The inky blackness of the night threw the glow of the pool lights up into our laps, making the two of us appear aqua-tinged and lolly-flavoured.

Yep, he looked lolly-flavoured alright.

'How did you do that, anyway?' I asked Jed.

'What?'

'You know. The talking-dog thing; the invite. I want it, and I don't even have a dog.'

'You haven't got this?' He got out his phone and pressed it, swiped the screen, but it didn't light up. 'I so need a new phone,' he said, throwing it down on the lounge. 'Friggin' thing. It's an app,' he went on. 'My mum had it; probably the first time she's shown me something on her phone that I thought was actually funny. Not the way she did it, of course – she just had him saying, "Hello, Jed. It's me, the Gun." But I could see the potential.'

'Show me,' I said, unlocking my phone and putting it in his hands.

He went to the App Store, found the app and passed the phone back to me.

'So if I download this,' I checked, 'the Gun will be able to talk to me?'

'Exactly.'

I grinned at him, bought it, then watched as the little circle started chasing itself.

Like a dog chasing its tail.

'So, now you take a photo.' Jed snapped a shot of the Gun looking at my phone, eyes tilted upwards. 'Then you line up the eyes and the mouth' – he moved the red dots and the dotted lines on the screen to match the Gun's face – 'and now he can say whatever you want.' Jed pressed the square red record button and leant forward into my phone and said, 'I like your nails, MC,' picking up one of my hands and holding it. 'They're very emo.'

The black polish still looked all glossy and perfect from the manicure I'd had earlier that day with Tosca.

Jed pressed replay and we watched as the Gun's mouth moved in sync with the words, saying to me, 'I like your nails, MC. They're very emo.' Press, repeat. 'I like your nails, MC. They're very emo.'

I felt, in that moment, as if I had captured Jed inside the mechanics of my phone. His voice, his dog, his stupidness, all there for eternity, for whenever I wanted to listen to him.

Like.

'I prefer the term "fully gothic",' I said, leaning over to the Gun and ruffling his fur.

Jed laughed. 'Vampire chic,' he said.

His knees were close to mine. His hand was folding the tips of my fingers into my palm, creating a soft fist, then letting go of the fist he'd created and running his hand over my wrist and back to my hand, like I was his.

I felt my breathing catch, my stomach filling up with butterflies. There was every chance that if I tried to speak, a brightly coloured, winged little something would flutter out from between my lips and go and settle on the nearest tree, instead of words.

'Vampire chic,' I said, testing my theory, then grinning at the fact that the butterflies had decided to stay inside my guts after all, pattering against my innards as they bumped into organs and settled on my ribcage.

The Gun was forgotten in that moment. Anouk was forgotten in that moment.

'I can roll with that,' I said.

'Vampira,' Jed said, then ran the edge of his fingernail down my throat to the little dip where the bones of my neck clicked into the front of my ribs.

The thinnest edge of his nail running the length of my throat.

I felt my chin lifting slightly, so his nail had full control of my throat. That's why vampires are so sexy – you lay your neck wide open and they drain you, possess you, taking your very breath away, and there's nothing you can do about it, because in the moment it feels so good that you don't care what the consequences are.

But I knew what the consequences would be. Anouk would be majorly pissed off if Jed and I kept going the way we were.

Not to mention the Gun, who was watching the two of us. This was going to freak the Gun right out.

'You know vampires aren't a real thing, don't you?' I said, clamping my chin back down, shutting my throat away and looking at Jed with a raised eyebrow.

The sensible side of me recognised that this here was the very last moment I could get up and go to the kitchen, grab a drink, start talking to someone else. Keep my friendship with Anouk safe.

I'd been warned – in French, no less. By a tram-riding, mermaid-swaying, wolf-eaten, peace-sign-flipping friend. I knew she wouldn't be happy if I stayed out here by the pool, with Jed's nail tracing the length of my neck.

But I didn't want to go inside. I didn't want another drink. I wanted to stay out here. I wanted to see what would happen. I wanted to feel what would happen, more importantly. Feel his mouth on mine, his hands on my body.

It was ages ago, the summer holidays, Merimbula, I felt like saying out loud, to the world, to Anouk. *Your dibs on Jed are past their use-by date.*

'The thing is,' I said, taking Jed's hand from my throat, 'I'm the one with the emo nails, not you, so even if vampires were real, you couldn't be one, because your fingernails' – and I held them up in front of his face – 'as you can see, aren't nearly vampire-y enough.'

He pushed his lips out, making a fish face. 'Not fair.'

No. It wasn't fair. Anouk had shotgunned him, but the fact was, he wasn't going anywhere near her. And his nail running down my neck? Well. It had been my neck he'd chosen, not Anouk's. How did a girl say no to that?

And look at him, with his handsome face and his gorgeous mouth.

'Luckily for you,' I said, remembering that the black nail polish Tosca-slash-Dad had bought me to match my manicure was still in my bag, 'I happen to have this little baby on me.' I held up the bottle. 'Vampire chic can be yours. For a price.'

He gave me a look that had all the butterflies rising in sync, as if he were the puppetmaster and his grin tugged all their strings; then when his smile relaxed, they all settled back down to my organs.

'Knock yourself out,' he said, and splayed his hands on my knees, his fingers spread like a starfish, ready for the polish.

Butterflies. Butter-friggin'-going-crazy-flies.

I twisted the brush out of the bottle and used the rim to bleed off the excess, then started running the brush the length of his nails, surprised at how hard it was to paint evenly. You'd think it would have been dead easy, but it wasn't.

He flicked one of his fingers under the hem of my skirt, then slid his eyes up at me, that naughty grin of his on his face.

'Stop that,' I said. 'I can't paint them properly if they're under my skirt.'

'That's a shit job you're doing,' he said, holding his hands up and looking at them. Some of the black was leaching onto the skin around the nails as well as being on the nails themselves.

'I think you'll find,' I said, bringing his hands back down to my thighs so I could keep painting (also, because it felt good having them there), 'that it's not actually me doing a shit job. It's the fact that you've got shit nails that makes it so hard.'

'Well, thank you.'

'That's my pleasure,' I said, trying to keep my hand steady as I applied slippery gloss to his middle finger.

He had long fingers, perfect nails. Even looking at his hands made some of the butterflies shiver – a tiny tremor down their microscopic spines. His skin, the bone structure underneath, it was all perfect.

'You know what annoys me about vampires?' I said, in a bid to distract myself from him – which was hard, seeing as it was only the two of us sitting there, by the pool, his hands on my thighs.

'What?'

'Well, it's actually impossible for teeth to just get long and pointy and then go back to being normal shape. There isn't an animal in the entire world that has teeth that change shape. If you're going to make up a terrifying monster, at least have it partly grounded in reality.'

'But you said if you painted my nails I'd become a vampire,' he said.

'Yeah, no. Not gonna happen.'

I finished his other hand and held his nails up for him, so he could survey my handiwork.

'Snakes,' Jed said finally.

'What?'

'Snakes have fangs that come down when they want to bite into something.' He turned his hands this way, then that, to get a better look at them. 'And then they retract. Therefore, consider your theory shut down. Just like that. Boom.'

'What theory?' Anouk asked, coming over and plunking herself down next to Jed on his banana lounge, her wolf hat looking toothy.

She picked up one of his newly black-nail-polished hands and raised her eyebrows at me, then put his hand back down on the seat beside her.

Squashing every single one of my butterflies under her arse.

What happened next was Anouk's suggestion.

Hers. Not mine.

'We should go for a swim,' she said, tilting her chin at Jed. 'How about how warm the water was in Merimbula?' Reminding the three of us that she still had first dibs on him.

Jed looked over at me. 'You feel like a swim?' he asked me.

I shook my head. 'I didn't exactly bring my bathers.'

I knew I should go inside, leave the two of them to it. But I felt unable to leave Jed's orbit. The feeling of his hands was still ghosted onto my thighs, holding me there.

'Well, so . . . what exactly are you wearing, then?' he asked, grinning at me.

I frowned at him. 'Is that a trick question?' I pulled at my T-shirt, in a clear demonstration of what exactly I was wearing.

'I meant underneath?'

My butterflies surged into a mob, flying blindly inside my stomach. The way he'd said 'underneath'.

But Anouk was sitting on the banana lounge next to Jed. She had his initials drawn into love hearts on her iPad cover. His name and hers were intertwined down the margins of her schoolbooks. She had dibs on him. In French.

'Just, you know, the usual,' I said, trying to act like it was completely innocent for Jed to be asking me what I was wearing underneath my clothes.

An everyday type of question.

A bit of banter between friends.

'Looks like you came fully prepared, then,' said Jed. 'I don't see a problem.'

Fully prepared? No. Swimming in my underwear with Jed and Anouk? No.

A little extra detail here for you, if I may. Anouk and I go to school together; I already told you that. We do gym together, and we've been in changing rooms together. Which means I know something about Anouk's underwear that you don't, and I'm going to share it with you now.

Although maybe I should let you in on a little something about my own underwear first, before I point out the little something about Anouk's.

The underwear I wear is completely normal. Plain. No lace, no crazy colours. Boy-leg pants and T-shirt bra in plain white or plain black are as exciting as I get in the underwear department. Anouk, on the other hand, has never stripped down in the school changing room to anything other than what could be described as hot tamale. I'm a Bonds girl (not Bond; Bonds). She's strictly Victoria's Secret online.

There was no way I could even vaguely compete with Anouk's Miranda Kerr angel-wings fluffy-feathers underwear. I stood up.

'I'm not really your skinny-dipping type,' I said, arms folded across my chest. 'I'll leave you guys to it.'

But Jed grabbed hold of my elbow and brought me back down to my banana lounge. 'How do you know if you've never tried it?' he asked me, his chin dipping as he tried to look in under my eyelashes.

'I can tell these things,' I said.

'But I think you've got the potential to be really good at it.' My heart jolted. 'Last swim of summer,' he said, and he peeled his T-shirt off and shucked his shorts down his legs.

It's so much easier for boys. Boxer shorts look exactly the same as board shorts.

'It's autumn,' I said, a churlishness clumping in my stomach as Anouk stood up in solidarity with Jed and slipped her skirt from her hips so it bunched on the ground at her feet, exposing lacy aqua-blue knickers. 'Officially autumn. Mid-autumn, in fact. Not traditionally swimming weather.'

'But it's still twenty-two degrees or something,' Jed said. 'It's definitely warm enough to have the last swim of summer.'

I didn't want to think about the moment when I'd pull my Radiohead T-shirt over my head and knock the world off its axis with my plain white bra; unzip my denim skirt and push it past my hips to the ground, to stand there in my don't-bother-staring-because-you-won't-get-a-big-thrill undies. And that wasn't the half of it. Once we were in the water, my plain white underwear was going to turn completely see-through. And then, after that, I'd have to get out of the pool, giving the world an opportunity to be blinded by my skinny white body as it was flashed at every single person I knew.

Photos to be taken. Posted wherever.

But Jed thought I had the potential to be good at it.

Butterflies, be still. Sit. Stay.

Although what guy wouldn't want to encourage two girls to strip down to their underwear and hop in the pool with him? No sane guy.

I looked around me, trying to find salvation somewhere. There was a bunch of towels on another banana lounge nearby. I grabbed one of them and held it to me. Wrapped it around my shoulders. Wriggled out of my Radiohead T-shirt. Unzipped my skirt.

I stood at the edge of the pool with my towel around me, Anouk on the other side of Jed in her aqua on aqua. Even the word 'aqua' sounded cooler, sexier, than 'white'. Jed held my hand, but he probably was holding Anouk's hand too; the three of us standing on the edge of the pool like paper cut-out dolls waiting to be mushed together when we hit the water.

I felt my breath sharpening, rasping inside my windpipe as I thought about jumping in.

I didn't want to do this.

I didn't want to be here.

But Jed thought I'd be good at it.

He counted, 'One, two ...' and on, 'three!' I watched from my side as Anouk jumped in, her arms stretched above her head in a 'V' for victory.

But I couldn't do it. Nothing victorious about me.

I stood by the edge of the pool, Jed still standing beside me, holding my hand.

'What are you doing?' he said, turning towards me. 'We had a deal.'

I shook my head. 'I can't. You go. I just don't, I can't. I'm too shy.'

I kept my towel wrapped firmly around myself, shielding my underwear and myself from scrutiny.

He put his hands on my shoulders and said low, so only I could hear him, 'You're not shy. I know you too well. There's nothing shy about you.' Which made me feel even shyer than if he'd said nothing. It was like he knew things about me that I didn't even know myself.

'Jump,' he said.

I shook my head.

'Jump,' he repeated.

I shook my head again.

He turned back to the pool and looked down at Anouk. 'How is it in there?' he asked, grinning.

'It's good. Warm. Why aren't you in here?' she said to him. Not looking at me. Her eyes studiously not looking at me.

He rubbed his hands up and down my arms, as if I needed warming up. 'She piked it,' he said.

Anouk swam over to the side of the pool and got out; wrapped a towel around herself, the scalloped edge of her aqua bra visible. She dried herself, grabbed her clothes off the banana lounge and bundled them into her arms. Put her wolf hat back on top of her damp hair. Padded, dripping, past us towards the house.

And into my ear as she walked past, in the quietest whisper, she said a little something especially for me: 'Thanks, friend.'

A snake-y hiss underlined her words. Draining my body like she was a vampire.

There were two ways I could go forward, from that moment. I could follow Anouk into the party and make sure she was okay. Apologise. Explain that I hadn't wanted to go in because I was wearing white undies that would go see-through as soon as they hit water.

Or I could stay outside with Jed, me wrapped in my towel, our clothes mushed up in a bundle on the banana lounge.

Let's be honest: I'd won. Not that it was a competition, but I'd won. Jed wanted to be with me. He couldn't have made it any clearer. The use-by date had expired. She couldn't say he was hers anymore.

Jed turned to face me, the lolly-blue of the pool echoing his eyes. 'You wanna go in?' he said. 'Apparently it's nice.'

Just the two of us. In the pool. The last swim of summer-officially-autumn.

Yeah, I wanted to go in.

I'd sort Anouk out later.

Chapter 4

That Sunday morning, I woke up to the back of Yumi's head.

I looked up at her ceiling, thoughts of Jed settling happily inside my head. I hadn't even brushed my teeth last night. Hadn't wanted to remove any Jed-ness from my body.

I could hear the rain outside, tapping against the window like there was a chance we might let it in.

It was lucky it hadn't rained last night. If it had rained, Jed and I wouldn't have sat by the pool. I wouldn't have painted his fingernails black. We wouldn't have gone swimming.

It had been so beautiful in there. Luke-warm bath temperature was how I'd described it to Jed. He'd laughed and said, 'Where's the soap?' then brought me in close to him. His body running the length of me. Our legs tangling, his skin merging into mine, his arms around me, his hands flat against my back, gripping me, feeling me, keeping me against him. I could feel, in the water, how much he wanted me. And I knew how much I wanted him. My plain white underwear, his boxer shorts, were the only thing separating us.

My heart thumped in my chest now even thinking about it.

I grabbed my phone from under the pillow and opened Insta to see if anyone had put up any new photos from last night yet. I knew they probably wouldn't have this early, but it was always worth checking.

They hadn't.

I went onto Snapchat and scrolled through a jumble of moments: Hattie and one of the girls from Saint Columba's, their arms around each other, raising their glasses to the camera; Hattie flopping out a rainbow tongue; Emile snapping a selfie of him and Yumi, his arm around her; another shot by Emile of Anouk with her hair wet, wolf hat on, towel around her shoulders, poking out her tongue like a cat. A video Yumi had put up, which made me laugh, of Liv and me doing dance-face – pouting our lips, narrowing our eyes, because the face you wear definitely makes a difference to how well you dance.

There were millions of photos of Jed, taken by pretty much everyone who'd been at his party, including a couple I'd uploaded of the two of us sitting outside by the pool together. Jed and Emile had posted multiple shots of the house after everyone had left, too: the kitchen bench piled with cans, lolly-blue pool visible through the back door; the Gun licking the kitchen floor to clean up the chip remnants; Mason, their other best mate, asleep on the couch with his eyebrows coloured in and a moustache drawn on.

'Stay,' Jed had said to me just before I'd left, his arms around me, holding me close.

'I can't,' I'd said, stepping back from him. 'You know what Yumi's dad's like. He's outside. I have to go.'

'Tell him you've changed your mind,' he said. 'Say you're staying at Hattie's. Or someone's. Somewhere. But stay here.'

Yumi's dad is our English teacher, and there isn't a thing you can get past him. He always picks us up from parties (or calls and speaks to whoever is supposed to be bringing us home), knows exactly what's going on, who's who and who shouldn't be hung out with. He's like your nightmare parent, except for the fact that he's really nice.

He'd only let us go to Jed's (no parents) on the condition that he came to pick us up at twelve o'clock, no arguments.

Damn you, Mr Yumi.

Of course his name isn't Mr Yumi. We just call him that. Actually, Yumi Yumi would be a cute name. Yumi should change her name to Yumi Yumi.

Hattie had posted a photo of her and Anouk back home after the party, the two of them lying in bed grinning up at the camera.

Anouk didn't look mad. That was a good thing.

I wondered what Anouk had said to Hattie when they'd got home. About me. About Jed. She couldn't be too mad. It wasn't really my fault. Jed had wanted to be with me; I couldn't help it if he wasn't into her. She'd had plenty of chances, months since she'd first been with him at Merimbula. He didn't want to be with her. It was as simple as that.

She'd be annoyed but she'd be fine.

I whispered into the back of Yumi's head, 'You awake?'

'No,' she mumbled.

'Liv. You awake?' I asked over Yumi's shoulder.

There was no answer from Liv's spot on the floor.

'Cute photo of you and Emile,' I said softly to Yumi.

Yumi flopped onto her back and took her phone off her bedside table then started scrolling, my head on her shoulder as she went through the various postings of last night's party, including a couple of shots Anouk had posted on Insta that I hadn't noticed when I'd scrolled through.

'Imagine if Jed and I start going out,' I said, lying back on the pillow and looking at the ceiling. 'Then we can go on double dates together. And then Liv can hook up with Mason …'

'There's no way,' I heard from the floor. 'I'm not ending up with Mason.'

Yumi and I both started laughing.

'But he's so sweet,' Yumi said. 'And he's not the ugliest guy in Year 12.'

'Close,' I said, 'but yeah, definitely not the ugliest.'

'If I wanted sweet, I'd go to the milk bar,' Liv said, climbing up onto the bed beside Yumi, squishing me against the wall.

'I could have had sex with Jed last night,' I said, biting down on my bottom lip. 'In the pool. God, I so wanted to.'

'Me too,' Liv said. 'With Mason.' And then she stuck her fingers down her throat.

'It doesn't matter if you're not into Mason,' I said. 'Imagine how much fun it would be for us all to go triple-dating.'

'Ain't gonna happen,' Liv said.

'Fine, then,' I said. 'Double dates are cosier anyway.'

'Anouk was pretty pissed off with you,' Yumi said, sitting up and resting her back against the head of the bed.

'Well, it's not my fault that Jed's into me. I mean, seriously, she can't keep dibs on him forever. He was so gorgeous. I seriously think we would have had sex in the pool, except for the whole house full of people,' I went on. 'I would have hated to get sprung.'

'The only thing worse than you being sprung would have been being the person who actually sprung you,' Liv said, pulling a vomit face to make her point.

Yumi put her hands over her mouth and started giggling. 'Omigod, I can't even believe I'm about to tell you this,' she said, shaking her head, then taking her hands away, a naughty grin opening her face, 'but, okay ... you know how we used to have a boat? Back when we were kids?'

I nodded. Not quite finished talking about Jed yet.

'So this one day, we took it out, right.' She was still grinning, her gaze fixed on the ceiling. 'Me and Mum and Dad and Wilder, and a few of their friends. And after we'd had lunch, we all got in the water to have a bit of a snorkel, and Mum and Dad put the paddleboard in the water, and whatever else they'd brought along.'

I nodded, not really understanding what on earth this had to do with anything, but captivated nonetheless. Yumi didn't talk about her mum much. The way she was giggling was making me start to laugh, even though she hadn't got to the funny part yet.

'So we're snorkelling, me and Wilder,' she went on. 'We're just kids, and we went a bit of a way from the boat, away from the others, and when I looked around I couldn't see anyone, but then I saw Mum and Dad in the water, their arms on the paddleboard, facing each other, talking. Right? So I started swimming over, yeah?

'And obviously they didn't know I was there, because they're talking to each other, looking at each other, and they think I'm off snorkelling nearer to the boat, so I had this idea that I'd swim underneath them and surprise them.'

Yumi started laughing fully now, hand over her face again, shaking her head like she shouldn't be saying any of this but she was on a roll now and just had to keep going.

'I swam under the water to them, and Mum's legs … I can't believe I'm telling you this, I'm still scarred … her legs were wrapped around Dad's waist, and as I got closer, I saw that neither of them had their bathers on, and I couldn't quite work it out because, you know, I was only a kid, so I went closer, and Dad's, well, basically, yeah, so, they're having sex, under the water, and I'm right there, snorkelling up to give them a surprise.' And then she stopped talking because she was consumed with laughter, the three of us were, heads thrown back on pillows, laughing our guts out at the thought of sweet, young, unscarred Yumi snorkelling up to get a close-up of her folks having sex.

'So, the thing is – my point is,' she finally managed to get out, 'if you and Jed had had sex in the pool last night, someone would have seen for sure. And they'd be scarred for life, right this moment, waking up this morning with the picture in their head of you and Jed having sex, never being able to get over it, never being able to look at you again without seeing that long sea creature going in and out—' And the three of us kicked our toes against the sheets with the gross hilariousness of it, until our legs were bare and the sheets were rumpled at our feet.

#

It stopped raining late in the afternoon. We went down to the skate park, because Yumi had a trick she wanted to nail, and Emile was going to show her how to land it. And since Emile was Jed's best mate, well ... maybe just maybe he might be there too.

'Hopefully Mason will be there too,' I said to Liv in the tram on the way there, elbowing her.

Liv bared her teeth at me like she wanted to bite me. Which was appropriate, because the T-shirt she was wearing had 'Bite Me' written across the front of it.

'Liv and Mason, sitting in a tree, K-I-S-S-I-N-G,' I sang.

Because I'm nothing if not immature.

'If I ignore you, you'll go away, right?' she said to me.

I shook my head. 'Not a chance.'

'Okay,' she said. 'Well, in that case ...' And she sat on me.

When we got there, Emile was on his lonesome. Just him and about a hundred kids all waiting to take their turns on the skate ramp.

No Jed.

Sigh.

Emile works down there at the skate park each Sunday, helping out when someone needs a hand, giving advice, explaining protocols to kids who are new to the ramp, demonstrating basic tricks for them, making sure everyone has a turn. He's a close-to-pro skateboarder, who figures he might as well get paid to hang out and do tricks.

When he saw Yumi, Emile dumped the kids like so many hot potatoes and came over to hang with us.

Ah, love.

Yumi wanted to land a tre flip, which means you bring your legs up, and the board comes with you, and then the board flips and lands back on the ground and your feet land on top of it and you keep going.

Very cool, if you can do it.

Very hard to nail, from the looks of it.

Yumi kept repeating the same movements over and over, popping the ollie, jumping off the board, landing too soon, stumbling, kicking the board, muttering to herself, not getting it, but nearly.

Emile stepped onto his board like it was a part of him, his knockabout old skater shoes hanging off the edge. He skated over to Yumi, telling her in his soft Moroccan accent, 'You need to have your back foot, your toes, hanging off the outside edge of the board so your foot kind of grabs it, so you can spin it three-sixty, and then your front foot is just going to be in normal kickflip position or whatever kind of feels comfortable.'

Then he kicked and flipped the board and landed and skated back to where Yumi stood watching him, chewing on her thumbnail.

And—

All kind of boring.

Liv had her phone out, and I took mine out, and we were both going through our feeds, the grinding of wheels against pavement creating white noise, blocking out the rest of the world. And that's when I noticed it. Not a thing, but an absence.

Nothing was coming through from Anouk.

I scrolled back up, but couldn't find any of her posts. It was like she'd gone offline. But Anouk would never go offline. She was the one, of any of my friends, who was always picking up her phone, checking Facebook, Insta, Snapchat, almost like a nervous habit; as if her hand literally needed something to hold on to in order to feel useful.

I remembered seeing her Insta posts on Yumi's phone that morning. But when I scrolled back, I couldn't find them.

Maybe she'd deleted her pics. Maybe she'd decided she didn't want to post about last night. I wondered if she was okay. About me. And Jed. And me and Jed.

I watched Yumi pulling her knees up, trying to flip her board, failing, looking pissed off, trying again.

I sent Anouk a peace offering: the photo I'd taken of her and Hattie on the tram going to Jed's party, both their hands held up in bunny ears, the universal sign for peace. My post of the photo, a peace sign from me to her.

I put it on Facebook. Tagged Hattie. Went to tag Anouk.

But there was no link to Anouk.

I looked at the photo, frowning.

My phone had been playing up a bit lately – sometimes it wouldn't ring, but then a message would come through that someone had just been trying to call. Texts were going missing. My battery was running flat really quickly. I definitely had a problem with my phone. Maybe that was why Anouk wasn't coming up.

But then I looked over Liv's shoulder to check what was coming through for her. Put my hand on her screen and scrolled through her Facebook feed.

And there it was. Stuff from Anouk. Photos. Comments. Likes. Everything exactly as you'd expect.

Just not to me.

'Omigod,' I said, my face flushing. 'Anouk's blocked me.'

Chapter 5

All that night, I couldn't get comfortable in bed. My arms got in the way. My legs felt itchy on the inside. My chest felt the weight of the doona against it. My shoulders felt the chill of the air.

Whereas the night before, at Yumi's, I'd slept the weighty bliss of the freshly kissed, that following night my mind flapped and hopped like a bird looking to nest, but finding nowhere safe.

I wanted to not-think about Anouk. I wanted to not-think about the next morning, walking into school, plonking myself down in the group on the quad and seeing how Anouk would react to me.

My mind kept circling, the word 'blocked, blocked, blocked' rotating inside my skull, bumping up against my very bones, making my head ache. How long did she expect someone not to kiss Jed if he wasn't into her? It was ridiculous to expect a person – say, for example, me – to not kiss Jed just because she still liked him. Also, what about the way Jed had been making a play for me over the past month or something? Every time we'd been at a party, he was always talking to me, making cute comments, leaning his arm against the wall next to my head and looking straight into me. It wasn't up to Anouk who Jed kissed. Jed had a say in it too. And so did I. I could kiss whoever I liked. I was single. Jed was single. We were both single. You can't actually dibs a person and expect them to be yours for the rest of your life, especially when you're NOT ACTUALLY WITH THEM.

I was going to pretend I hadn't realised she'd blocked me.

I was going to walk into school the next morning and act like everything was completely normal.

I was going to say 'hi'. Not notice that she was kind of shitty.

Ignore, ignore, ignore.

It would be fine. Things always seemed worse at night. Something about the darkness seemed to illuminate every-thing you didn't want to think about.

Blocked, blocked, blocked, blocked, blocked, blocked, blocked, blocked.

It didn't help that Jed hadn't liked any of my Insta shots all day. Hadn't responded to my post where I'd recorded new words to go with the photo I had of the Gun, saying, 'Great party – my voice is feeling *husky* today,' – which, you have to admit, was a pretty good dog pun.

I'd even poked him, which, I don't know, who even pokes these days? But it had seemed like a good idea at the time.

At three o'clock in the morning, I had full poke regret.

It had made me seem too keen. So, I picked up my phone and unpoked him. And instantly had unpoke regret. If he'd seen my poke, then noticed that I'd unpoked him, it would look bad. But maybe he hadn't seen my poke and that was why he hadn't poked back.

I shouldn't have poked him in the first place.

I remembered he'd said he needed a new phone on Saturday night. That it was always dying. Maybe it really had died, for good this time, and he wasn't able to see any of my posts.

His folks needed to get him a new phone so I wouldn't have to go through all this angst.

Also, I'd been with him plenty of times when he'd taken his phone out and scrolled through a screen filled with icons: text messages and missed calls and What'sApp and Insta notifications and whatever. He often had his phone switched to silent. He wasn't a phone-checker. He was one of those non-phone-checker types.

But he and Emile had posted all those shots after everyone had left. And surely, if you have a party, you want to see what everyone posts about it afterwards. Even a non-phone-checker wants to see the verdict of their own party.

His phone must have died. That was the only answer.

My mind flopped back to Anouk. Then flipped back to Jed. It even fluttered around Emile for a while, thinking back to how he'd been that day at the skate park. Had he seemed slightly uncomfortable? Had Jed said something to him after I'd left the party, and now Emile had to go through that awkward phase of having his girlfriend's friend liking his friend and his friend not liking her back?

Although I already knew Jed wasn't the puppy-dog keen type. It's not like I would have expected him to call me the next day and be slobbering all over me. He wasn't that type of guy.

But he could have poked me back.

Except no one poked anymore. It had been a bad move on my part. Why had I poked him? I shouldn't have poked him.

At least my post with the Gun had been cute, funny. How hard would it have been to put a simple 'haha' comment underneath it? Although maybe it was a bit copycat-ish. He'd used the Gun to invite everyone to the party, and then I'd used the Gun to say thanks. Maybe he'd thought it didn't make sense.

I picked up my phone and deleted the post with the Gun on it. Then regretted it. I should have left it up there. It was cute. It was funny. I should have left it.

And then, how about Anouk blocking me?

Which brought my flapping mind circling back to the beginning again, cawing and squawking over the juicy worms that were crawling inside my brain.

There was no milk for breakfast on Monday morning. Also no bread to make a sandwich; and only Pizza Shapes, which I don't like, for my snack, and one cruddy apple.

Not only had Mum given up on the whole cooking business since Dad had moved out; she also seemed to have forgotten the whole shopping idea as well.

76

'There's literally nothing to eat,' I said to her as I slammed the fridge door shut.

Harley came into the kitchen, looked in the fridge, then went back out.

'Get some money out of my wallet, run to the milk bar and grab some milk and bread,' Mum said, towel-drying her hair, 'then I'll pick stuff up from the supermarket on my way home from work tonight. Or Harley can. Harley,' she called after him, 'can you go up the street and get some stuff?'

No answer.

Mum works every Monday and Thursday at Maude's homewares shop. The rest of the week, she's entirely and utterly free to do whatever else it is she does with her days. Which evidently no longer included the shopping.

'Why is it so hard to get things, you know, bought around this house?' I stewed. 'Besides, I can't go to the milk bar, because if I do I'm going to miss the tram, and then I'll be late for school.'

Magic words, those. As soon as I'd said them out loud I recognised them for the gold they were. I went over to Mum's bag and fished out her wallet.

'So long as you know that when you get sent a late notice for me from school this morning,' I called back at her from the front door, 'it's all your fault ...'

And I slammed the door shut.

Getting to school late was the perfect plan, because it meant that I wouldn't have to suffer through that initial walk of shame up to the quad and have everyone notice that Anouk wasn't talking to me.

I sent Liv a text saying I wouldn't be able to catch the tram with her. Then I took my good old time walking to the milk bar, wandered the aisles (admittedly that only took up a minute or so; it's a small milk bar), stood at the fridge trying to decide what sort of milk I should be getting (did we normally have low-fat or normal – who knew?), got sugary white bread because Mum never bought it but if I was buying I was going to get the stuff that was bad for me, bought myself a pack of Twisties for my snack (ditto on the bad stuff), then took my good old time wandering back home again.

Sat and ate my breakfast.

Scrolled through my phone. Checked that Anouk had really, definitely, absolutely blocked me. Yep. Nothing there.

I figured if I could get through today, everything would be fine. She couldn't hold a grudge forever.

It'd only last a day or two, I said to myself.

Fly away, little birdie who knew nothing. Fly away. Little did I know that today was only the start of everything getting very, very much worse.

#

As I sat down with everyone in the quad at morning break, Anouk slid her eyes over at me for the first time that day. She made sure I saw her seeing me, then she turned away, so that I was a hundred per cent sure that I was being ignored.

She'd noticed me all right, though. She'd made an extra-special point of noticing me, of registering my presence, of looking straight at me, and then she'd deliberately turned away from me, making sure I was crystal clear that I was being ignored.

Maybe 'shunned' is a better description.

A lumpen Twistie snagged in my throat. I'd known this snub was coming, but it still managed to clamp my gullet in like a gym-bag with its strings drawn tight.

It wasn't until we were walking into the last class of the day, English with Mr Yumi, that I was able to say anything to her. It was as if everyone had made a silent pact to position themselves between us, through every break of the day, every class we shared, making it geographically impossible for me to talk to her until now.

I touched her on the elbow as we walked through the door, just lightly, as if she was an invalid, and said to her, 'Hey, I know you're probably a bit annoyed that I was with Jed at the party. But, you know ...' And I left it at that, because honestly, I wasn't sure what to say next. She just needed to join the dots, and the dots were obvious; they were like gigantic black circles in front of her face. She couldn't miss the dots.

She turned to me, her feet solid in the doorway. I realised that saying something to her at exactly the moment that we would create a bottleneck of rubberneckers had been a bad move. I tried to pull her towards me, out of the way of the door, but she stood firm.

'I couldn't give a shit that you were with Jed,' she said, the words blowing harsh against my face. 'If you think that's what this is about, then you're more pathetic than I realised.'

I blinked at her.

'You know what, MC? If you're so desperate to be with him, go for it. Go paint his nails. So *cute*.' Sarcasm, ladies and gentlemen, is alive and well. 'But the fact that you deliberately stopped him jumping in the pool with me – in my UNDERWEAR, by the way, in case you hadn't noticed … the fact that you didn't come in too … well, if that's the kind of friend you are, MC, I can do without you as a friend.'

Mr Yumi, sensing a problem, uttered a stern, 'Girls!' to get us to move out of the doorway.

'I didn't stop him,' I hissed, keeping my voice quiet in the utterly useless hope that no one would notice what was going on. 'Besides, he's the one who asked me to paint his nails. Not the other way around.'

Okay, the nail thing had been my idea, but that kind of detail wasn't going to help matters.

'And then,' she said, her books held against her chest like a war shield, 'because you're a prize bitch—'

'Annick. MC,' Mr Yumi called over from his desk. 'Girls. I'm about to start class.'

But Anouk went on, because everyone was listening now: '—it's only once I get out of the pool that you decide, *Oh yeah*,' – and here she put on a simpering imitation of what was definitely *not* my voice – '*maybe I will go for a swim with you after all, Jed. Now that Anouk's gone inside, a swim sounds like a really fun idea.* You want Jed? You can fucking have him.' The brutality in her voice for those last words was a stark contrast to the limpness when she'd imitated me.

'Annick!' Mr Yumi said. 'Desk. Now. One more word and I'll send you to the principal's office.'

'That's not how it was,' I said. 'I didn't—'

'MC, I said that's enough,' Mr Yumi said.

'Every time we've gone to a party lately,' Anouk went on, not even caring that Mr Yumi had now come over and was standing over the two of us, 'you've been all over him like a rash. It's embarrassing. I feel embarrassed for you. Everyone's laughing behind your back. I'm the only one who's game to say it to your face.'

'Okay, Annick,' Mr Yumi said. 'I told you one more word. Principal. Now.'

'I haven't,' I said. '*He's* been—'

'One more word, MC,' barked Mr Yumi. 'I'm serious. Maybe the two of you could sort this out in Mrs Willis's office.'

I went over and sat down at my desk. Slammed my books down. The last place I wanted to be was sitting out the front of Mrs Willis's office with Anouk, just the two of us.

Anouk left, slamming the door.

I sat through the entire class not hearing a single word Mr Yumi said. I didn't even feel like calling him Mr Yumi anymore. Not even inside my head.

Mr Martin.

I was going to call him Mr Martin from now on, for the rest of my life. Even when I went over to Yumi's place, I'd call him Mr Martin. Formal. Distant. I'd never forgive him for not letting me say what I'd wanted to say.

For leaving Anouk with the last word.

I felt the weight of all that Anouk-ness on my shoulders. I was amazed at how heavy it was. It crowded out everything else.

She's only one person, I told myself as I sat through English. There was still Liv and Yumi and Hattie and everyone else I could talk to; I didn't have to worry about Anouk.

Fuck Anouk.

Fook Anouk.

Go have a sook.

I played over, like a gif, the moment she'd looked at me and said, *Thanks, friend.* Loop. *Thanks, friend.* Loop. *Thanks, friend.* Then I shook it up a bit, by replaying the moment just before, in front of everyone in class, when she'd said, *You've been all over him like a rash. It's embarrassing. I feel embarrassed for you.*

Over and over, on repeat.

Thanks, friend. Embarrassed for you. Thanks, friend. Embarrassed for you.

Thanks, friend.

Embarrassed for you.

\#

'I can't believe she said I'm the one who's been all over Jed,' I said to Liv on the tram on the way home.

Liv ran her hand through her hair as if to push it off her face, even though when your hair is as short as Liv's, you hardly need to worry about it falling into your eyes.

'I mean, seriously,' I went on, 'he's the one who's been all over me, not the other way around. In fact – and this is what really pisses me off – at all the other parties, when I could have kissed him, I always walked away. Because I didn't want to HURT HER FEELINGS. And now she's acting like I'm the bitch who's been trying to get onto him all this time. And making out like I was flirting by painting his finger-nails, which was nothing – just, you know, mucking around. I mean, if anything, *I'm* embarrassed for *her*, not the other way round. Jed and I were sitting out by the pool, on our own, and then she comes out and sits with us, and says, *Let's have a swim*. I don't feel bad at all. Who does that, comes over when two people are on their own outside, obviously kind of having a nice time by themselves? Who does that? No one, that's who. You know what? Bad luck. Bad luck that she liked him. It's over, move on, go have a sook.'

'She'll get over it,' Liv said, her feet on the tram seat beside me. 'She's just pissed off.'

'Yeah, well, she didn't need to take it out on me. In front of everyone. I mean, Jesus, who does that shit? You've seen Jed with me before; you've seen how he hangs around me. It really pisses me off that she then flips everything to make out like I'm the one hanging off him. If anyone was a bad smell, it was her. I mean, seriously, that was embarrassing when she said that whole thing about Gregory Peck, don't you reckon?'

Liv frowned a little. 'I don't know about the Gregory Peck thing.'

I stared at her. 'Are you joking? When we were round at Yumi's before Jed's. How could you *not* have heard her? You know, we were watching *Roman Holiday*? And Wilder was laughing because we were all crying – well, except *you* – and she said she was crying because Gregory Peck reminded her of Jed. Even though they look nothing alike.'

'Oh, right.'

'You know. Before the party?'

'Yeah. I didn't hear it. I can't remember. Anyway, she'll get over it. Don't worry about it.'

I felt a stammer inside my head. How could Liv not have heard Anouk's comment about Gregory Peck? She was there. In the room.

'You know, just before we went upstairs to get dressed,' I pressed.

'Yeah.' Liv shook her head. 'I don't know. I'm not saying she didn't say it. I just didn't hear it.'

That annoyed me. She must have heard Anouk. Anouk had been so obvious. 'And like I said,' I continued, 'I'm really pissed off that she made out like I've been chasing Jed, when he's totally been after me all this time.'

'Yeah.'

'She's always had a problem with me,' I went on, chewing on my lip and feeling more and more outraged at the unfairness of it. 'Ever since I started at Whitbourn.'

Even though I've known Yumi since we were in kinder, and Liv ever since we moved in next door to her in Grade 2, I hadn't started at Whitbourn Grammar with the two of them until Year 9, when I was awarded a scholarship.

That first year at Whitbourn, we had to do a project for health class that we worked on at our own pace. Everyone did something different – choosing whatever it was they were interested in – and we had to regularly update our progress on our own blog. One of the girls trained for months to do a twenty-one-k mini-marathon. Yumi built a skateboard.

I did this thing where I got photos of celebrities then erased all their make-up, pulled their hair back in a ponytail, dressed them in normal clothes, and photoshopped them into different street scenes with normal people, as a way of showing that celebrities, when you strip everything back, are the same as all of us.

Political statement, consider yourself made.

Anyway, at the end of the year there was a prize for the most popular blog. And Anouk got shortlisted.

She'd fostered a seeing eye dog, a puppy, and her year-long project had been to train him and care for him, bring him to school, take him everywhere with her, and at the end of the year, give him back to the seeing eye dog people, so they could finish his training and give him to a blind person.

Of course her blog was super-popular. It had a puppy in it. What did you expect? And hey, props to her.

But on the day the shortlist was announced, when I gave her a hug and said how well she'd done, how much she deserved those props, she looked at me all fake-modest, and said in her best fairy-floss voice, 'God, no, I'm so shocked I'm on the list.' And then she'd added, 'I mean, I can't believe you didn't get shortlisted.' And yeah, inside myself I was secretly a bit disappointed too, but it wasn't really a big deal. But *then* she'd added, 'And you didn't even make the longlist, which you definitely should have.'

Longlist? I hadn't even known there was a longlist.

That was the day I recognised that the competition I'd felt between Anouk and me was real; that I hadn't been imagining it. There'd been other small things here and there, but that little dig about me not even getting on the longlist, that was when I knew for sure.

'And I mean, if things were the other way around,' I went on now to Liv, as the tram rumbled along its tracks, 'I wouldn't go all psycho about it. I get that she's upset Jed's not into her, but she doesn't need to go off at me about it. That's got nothing to do with me.'

'Yeah.'

I could hear how boring I was being; the way I kept picking at the same thoughts like they were scabs. But I needed to vent, and Liv was my ventee. That was the deal we had: if one of us ever felt like being the venter, the other would be the ventee.

That. Was. The. Deal.

I opened my phone and checked to see if there was anything from Jed yet. Anything. A like or a comment or a something. A photo of the two of us. Something. Just anything. But there was a whole lot of nothing from him.

A thought slotted into my brain like a coin in a drink machine.

'You don't think,' I said, testing the waters of the universe with my little toe, 'that I shouldn't have been with Jed, do you? I mean, what if ...' What if it meant nothing to him?

Liv looked straight at me. 'No,' she said, her arms folded over her schoolbag. 'Nuh. Definitely not. He likes you. You and Jed have always got on really well. Don't worry about it. Everything'll be fine. Anouk will get over it.'

But now that the thought had clattered into my head, it was clanking around like so much loose change.

Imagine if I'd wrecked my friendship with Anouk over a guy.

And then the guy never called.

#

We got off the tram and walked down our street, me peeling off at my house and Liv continuing on to hers next door.

I went upstairs to my room and opened my secret Tumblr account.

I hadn't looked at it for a good couple of years. I'd started it when I moved to Whitbourn; agirlwalksintoaschool, I'd called it. A little secret something I'd never told anyone about.

Even though I'd already met quite a few of the girls at Whitbourn through Liv and Yumi before I'd started there, it had taken a bit of getting used to, the whole single-sex thing, and agirlwalksintoaschool had been my secret way of sorting things out in my head – and much safer than a diary. A diary hidden in my desk drawer could have been found and read by anyone, but my blog on Tumblr, while in a way being the world's most public diary, was hidden in the wood of millions of gig of data. No one I knew could ever find it. Ever.

Looking back over the old posts, I saw that Whitbourn had taken a lot more getting used to than I'd remembered:

'Hattie is ALWAYS talking about boys – blah blah blah, boys boys boys. It's like she's never met a boy before. God, Hattie, THEY'RE JUST GUYS!'

And: 'Everyone ACTS like they're all really friendly with me, but this weekend Annick's having EVERYONE for a sleepover' – she was Annick back then; this was before the emergency teacher called her Anouk – 'and it's only because Liv said something to her that she asked me, last-minute, to come too. Yeah, thanks Annick. Real nice, EXCLUDING THE NEW GIRL.'

And: 'I'm not going to catch the tram with Liv tomorrow. She's being AN ABSOLUTE bitch – I think we might need to move house.'

Even Yumi wasn't immune: 'Yumi always kind of CHECKS with Liv about whether or not she should do something. Like, MAKE UP YOUR OWN MIND, Yumi! That's what it's there for.'

Clearly capital letters were big for me in Year 9.

But then I'd settled in at Whitbourn, and everyone had got used to me being there, and I'd stopped going on Tumblr because I didn't have anything major to vent about.

On this particular day, however, after Anouk had been such a heinous bitch, creating a new Tumblr post was exactly what I needed.

'Girls can be bitches,' I wrote. 'Most of the time they're great – some of my best friends are girls; hell, I'm even a girl – but, yeah, girls can be real bitches. And Anouk is Numero Uno in that department.'

I stopped for a moment, unsure what to say next, feeling a zing of danger. If Anouk ever saw this, I'd be dead. Dead. But she'd never see it, because no one knew agirlwalksintoaschool existed except me.

Well, okay, me and my twenty-five random followers. Popular? Me? Hells yeah!

'She's got this cute Nordic name, which makes you think of skiing and snow and saunas, but don't be fooled. Vikings came from Norway. And trolls. And there are probably a whole lot of other scary people from Norway who I can't think of right this moment. Norway isn't as great as you think it is.'

I paused, then added: 'No offence to all you Norwegians out there.' No point pissing off a whole nation of people.

'But,' I went on, 'she's acting like me kissing this guy is the worst thing that's ever happened in the history of the world, and it's totally not. Also, Anouk, if a guy wants to kiss me, and I want to kiss him, then I should be allowed to. I don't need your permission. He's not yours. You don't own him. He didn't want to be with you. Get over it. Get over yourself. I can't believe you blocked me. And then spent the entire day ignoring me. With friends like you, who needs enemies? Jesus, what a bitch.'

And then I pressed post.

Feeling satisfyingly vented.

Chapter 6

That Thursday, after nearly an entire school week of Anouk not talking to me, Dad rang.

'I've decided to move out of Grandpa's,' he said down the phone.

Finally. Something going right.

I still hadn't heard from Jed – big fat nothing. Nada. A whole lot of no-Jed. And Anouk with her no-talking was also taking up a big chunk of my headspace. It was crazy how much room two not-speaking people could take up.

But at least now, with Dad moving back home, I'd be back to some kind of normal. Me, hip-and-shouldering him out of the way of the toaster in the morning. Me, brushing my hair because I was a perfect daughter, no wreck of the *Hesperus* here. Me, putting my iPad down every night when he came in the door and having a chat with him about my day, his day, every day. The four of us sitting down to dinner every night. Harley not slamming around the house anymore. Everything back to normal.

'Well,' I teased him, 'you'll have to do a fair bit of grovelling, but I suppose we'll let you move back. You can try buying my affection back with clothes, for example. I've seen these really nice jeans, in case you're wondering.'

There was a beat of silence before Dad filled the void slowly, carefully, like he was treading into a watery conversation and he wasn't sure how far he was going to sink. 'Oh. No, MC, darling, no, sorry, I didn't mean that. I meant, I've found this great house. And it's just around the corner from you and Harley – so close, you'll love it. I'm moving in this weekend. I thought you might like to come help me set up your new bedroom. We can grab some takeaway for dinner. It'll be fun.'

Dad staying at Grandpa's had always seemed like a temporary situation. A whole new house was going to make it so much harder for him to move back home to us.

'Oh.' My room blurred as my eyes filled with tears. 'Yeah, no, sure, that sounds great. Okay, Dad, well, I gotta go, I've got lots of homework to do.'

'Whatever you want,' he rushed into the conversation before I hung up. 'Pizza. Thai. Whatever you want. Your choice.'

No, it wasn't my choice. Because my choice wouldn't have been for either of those things; my choice would have been for him to be back home with us. But that wasn't going to happen.

I pressed the red button and ended the call.

Because what else was there for me to do?

#

That Saturday afternoon, while Dad drove to get the key from the real estate agent, I hung with Grandpa, eating a sandwich he'd made me: thin white bread with butter, finely sliced tomatoes and salt and pepper.

Another of Grandpa's sandwich specialties is vegemite and grated apple. Or thinly sliced cucumber, salt-and-peppered.

It's strangely tasty, in an old-person way.

'You're a good girl, helping your dad move,' Grandpa said, filling the kettle with water and putting it on the stove.

'Yeah,' I said, chowing down on the sandwich, 'I'm a legend. He owes me.'

Grandpa smiled, taking a couple of cups and saucers out from the cupboard: finely floral bone china, the cups with curled handles, making a delicate clinking noise when he put them onto the saucers.

'How's Harley going?' he asked, taking out the teapot and scooping wisened tea-leaves into it.

What he really wanted to say was, *What's going on with Harley? Why don't I see him anymore?* But Grandpa was never one to come at something head-on; he was much more gently, gently in his approach. Not like his granddaughter, who sat on the tram and spewed venom to her ventee when she was upset.

Different generations.

The kettle boiled. Grandpa poured water into the teapot, left it on the bench to steep – that's what he said, 'I'll just leave that to steep a minute' – and then sat back down at the table with me.

'Harley's fine,' I said.

Although who knew? I couldn't really tell. All I knew was that he didn't hang out with Wilder anymore, he acted strangely with me, was hardly ever home, and wasn't talking to Dad.

'Bring him with you next time you come over,' Grandpa said.

As if Harley would trot along behind me like an obedient dog.

'For sure, Grandpa,' I said. 'Definitely.'

Grandpa chewed carefully on his sandwich, as if he didn't want to dislodge any teeth. Then he pushed back from the kitchen table and stood up.

'I've got something to show you,' he said, walking out of the room and coming back in with a photo album. 'I was looking through this the other day.'

He opened the album and pointed at various photos, the wonky top-joint of his finger making me feel wistful and sad because it made me realise that things change and there's nothing you can do about it.

Even fingers change. Shift out of shape.

I looked at photos of Harley and me in pyjamas lifting our freshly unwrapped Christmas presents up above our heads so they could be snapped in all their glory by the camera; Harley sitting on Mum's knee; me sitting on Dad's; me lying as a three-year-old flat on top of Grandpa as he lay on the couch and tried to snooze; Harley scrunching up the newspaper as he sat on Grandy's knee.

'When Grandy died,' Grandpa said, tapping with his crooked finger on the photo of Grandy and Harley, 'remember how you both stayed the night to keep me company? We all slept together in my bed, and you both talked through all the things you loved about her until we fell asleep.'

I felt tears come unexpectedly into my eyes. I didn't need to think back over sad times – I was living through plenty-enough sad times right this moment.

'That first night,' he said, and his chin rumpled like an old sheet, 'that very first night, you both made me laugh with the things you said. I cried a lot, but I laughed a little, too.'

I took another bite of my tomato sandwich, hoping the bread would soak up the sadness that seemed to be welling inside my mouth.

'My point is,' he went on, 'sad things happen. And you don't know when you're going to feel better. But you will. You're going through a bit of a rough trot at the moment; you and Harley both are: Mum and Dad breaking up, Dad now moving into a new house. But everything will get better. I promise you. It always does.'

He patted me on my shoulder.

I didn't answer. Just kept on trying to swallow the clump of chewed-up, damp, tomatoey bread.

\#

Dad's new house was a lace-trimmed weatherboard cottage, freshly painted, with a rose climbing along the verandah. Pretty, was the word that sprang to mind.

Pretty. Sweet. Lovely.

Dad's house. It felt strange thinking it. His own separate digs. While he'd been at Grandpa's, it had still felt like we were keeping him in the family. We were still all together, but slightly apart. But now, with him moving into his own house, just him on his own, I worried that he was in danger of sliding off down side streets and freeways and away, away, away from us.

I'd just finished sorting out my bedroom – new bed, new pillows, new doona, new sheets, new bedside table, new lamp; ditto on the new bed et cetera for Harley (good luck with that, I felt like saying to Dad, as I was pretty sure Harley wasn't going to be sleeping there anytime soon) – when there was a knock on the front door.

Dad stopped in my doorway on his way to answer it. 'You've done a good job,' he said, hugging me to him and kissing the top of my head. 'Hungry?'

'Starving.'

'You go get the dishes. I'll get the pizza.'

His first guest: the pizza guy. It seemed very single-dad-ish, and I felt lonely for him. Every night he was going to be here on his own, without me, without Harley or Mum, without even Grandpa for company.

I went into the kitchen and took out knives and forks. Plates. And then I looked up as Dad and the pizza guy came into the kitchen.

Only it wasn't the pizza guy.

'I wasn't sure what to get,' Tosca said, holding white plastic bags aloft, bracelets clinking, the house filling with the smell of green curry and whatever else she had in there. 'So I got a selection.'

I stared at her. Then at Dad.

'I thought you said pizza,' I said.

'Oh no,' Tosca said. 'That's my fault. Sorry. I just thought … there's this great little Thai place around the corner, and I thought … but I can organise pizza if you'd rather that.'

'Thai's great,' Dad said. 'Pizza. Thai. It's all the same thing.'

It definitely wasn't. There is no need to explain to anyone, not a single living person, that there is a definite difference between pizza and Thai.

The fact was, I didn't even like pizza that much.

I preferred Thai.

But he'd said pizza.

He'd. Said. Pizza.

I put the two plates away, and got two bowls out instead.

Two bowls. One for me. One for Dad.

Dad got out a third bowl and put it beside our two. 'What about Tosca?' he said.

'Oh,' Tosca said, shaking her head, her earrings jingling. 'No. It's nice for you guys to enjoy the new house together on your first night, just the two of you.'

Yes. I agreed.

'I can't expect you to turn up with food,' Dad said, opening the cupboard (that I'd packed) and pulling out a couple of wine glasses (that I'd unpacked), 'and then not invite you to stay. You have to stay. You can help us warm the new house. The more the merrier.'

I looked at the two of them. Standing in Dad's pretty little house with all his new stuff.

The only remnant of his old life, in the entire house, was stupid old me.

Chapter 7

Two weeks later, Liv and I were over at Yumi's place. Wilder was sitting at the kitchen table, trawling through Tinder, swiping right, swiping left, swiping right.

The three of us looked over his shoulder. Yumi rested her arm on his back to better see the yes-please-swipe-rights and the sorry-you're-definitely-lefts he was scrolling through.

There was Rachel, standing in the kitchen wearing one of those masks you can buy from the newsagent, a gold cardboard masquerade mask. Twenty-eight years old, apparently, although it was hard to tell with the mask on. Eight kilometres away; active two weeks ago. 'Not looking for anything serious, but definitely happy for something fun.'

Wilder swiped right.

'Twenty-eight?' Yumi said. 'You don't think she's a little old for you?'

'I've gone flexi on my age limits. I'm seeing what's out there.'

Sue, twenty-two, was four kilometres away, active one day ago, with pink hair, green nails. 'Not even sure I should be on Tinder. I don't want a fling, so if that's what you're after, I'm not your girl.'

He swiped right.

'Hang on,' Yumi said to him. 'Rachel wants nothing serious, and Sue's *not* interested in a fling? You ever heard the term "mixed messages"?'

Wilder shrugged. 'I'm in a right-swipe kind of mood,' he said.

There was a girl riding a photoshopped unicorn; a girl with rainbow-coloured hair; a girl wearing a hamburger outfit, whose 'About' section read, 'I don't have avian flu.'

Right swipe, right swipe, right swipe.

'The girl in the hamburger suit is cute,' Yumi said.

'She's definitely the best so far,' I agreed.

'*And* she doesn't have avian flu,' Liv said. 'Which has got to be a bonus.'

And then the next face scrolled up: Julie, thirty-five, six kilometres away, active one day ago. A woman who I knew for a fact wasn't thirty-five, more like forty-something, with a glass of wine in her hand and a hopeful smile on her face, wearing a gold silk shirt with a couple of long silver chains dangling down her cleavage.

Mum.

I felt Wilder hesitate for the smallest second, his finger hovering over the screen, not sure what to do. Because, of course, Wilder knew exactly who she was. I could almost hear the cogs in his brain turning over as he thought to himself, *Hang on a sec, that's Harley's mum*, and then a *clunk* as the next thought dropped into his head of, *and MC's mum*, and then, *whirr-click*, the clincher of, *so do I swipe right or do I swipe left?*

There's no easy way to move past a person on Tinder. You have to either right-swipe for 'like', or left-swipe for 'no thanks'. That's how it works. And while Wilder hesitated, me, Yumi and Liv were all left staring at Mum's face.

'Left swipe,' I said, stepping back from him. 'Jesus. Put us all out of our misery. Left swipe. Left, left, left.'

I walked out of the kitchen, Yumi and Liv coming up behind me, the two of them putting their arms around my shoulders as we walked up the stairs to Yumi's bedroom.

None of us saying a word.

I flopped down on Yumi's bed and put my arm over my eyes, shaking my head. I knew they were both watching me. Their stillness filled the room with noise, as they tried to think of the best thing to say.

I took my arm away from my eyes and looked over at them. Yumi was leaning against her desk, watching me, her hands resting on the desktop. Liv was sitting on Yumi's desk chair – yep – watching me.

'Let's make a pact,' I said, putting my hands up in surrender, 'that we never mention this ever again.'

'Fair enough,' said Yumi.

'Ever.'

'For sure,' said Liv.

Yumi hunkered down and took an album out of its sleeve, laid it on the turntable, lifted the needle and placed it on the outer edge of the grooves. She handed the cover to me, giving me something to do, something to occupy my eyes, occupy my brain, then started flicking through her collection, working out which one she'd put on next.

That's the thing with records. You have to change them every half-hour or so, because that's how long a side lasts. It's kind of annoying, but also kind of nice. Every twenty minutes, you have to think about what you want to listen to next, instead of all the songs blurring into one another, which is what happens when I listen on my phone.

The album cover Yumi had passed to me was Tom Waits. I wouldn't even know who Tom Waits was, except that Yumi has four of his albums, each of them with 'Lucy Blue' written in the top right-hand corner in neat, sixteen-year-old-girl writing. Purple biro.

Lucy Blue. Yumi's mum, before she married Yumi's dad.

She would have been about my age, our age, when she signed her name on the album, marking it as hers.

And now she's not even around anymore.

Just like that. Dead.

I watched Yumi flip the cover of the album she was considering playing next and study the song list, chewing on the inside of her mouth as we listened to Tom's gravelly voice.

'Thirty-five,' I finally said, shaking my head. 'Apparently she's thirty-five. News to me.'

And suddenly all three of us were laughing, tears rolling down our faces.

'Okay,' I managed to get out, shaking my head, still laughing, 'that's probably the most embarrassing thing that's ever happened to me. Ever. In my life.'

'No way,' Liv said, a broad grin on her face. 'You've had way more embarrassing things happen than that.'

'Name one.'

She glanced over at me, grinning. 'Welllll …' She scratched her eyebrow. 'Hang on a minute; just give me a sec …'

'Exactly. Definitely the most embarrassing thing that's ever happened. In my entire life.'

We started laughing again.

'It's just me and Wilder and Liv,' Yumi pointed out. 'It's not that embarrassing.'

'It's not you guys I care about. It's me. Having to see that. That's the type of thing that can traumatise a person forever. I can never scrub my eyes clean.'

'Poor Wilder,' Yumi said, jumping up to sit cross-legged on top of her desk and grinning at me. 'That'd be the first time he's broken into a sweat over a girl in a long time.'

'I don't ever want to go home again,' I said, 'and face my mum knowing this. I mean, seriously. Gross.'

'I guess that's what parents do when they split up,' Yumi finally said.

'Yeah. I guess.'

And suddenly I realised it wasn't funny at all. Dad had a new house. He had Tosca.

Mum had Tinder.

In order for Dad to have the life he wanted, Mum had to have a life she didn't want. We all did. Me and Mum and Harley.

It was like a cosmic seesaw.

Dad's up required all of our downs.

Chapter 8

It was one of those late-autumn, coming-up-to-winter weekends where the weather had decided it'd had enough of us hanging around outside and was all: *Don't even think about bothering me again for at least a good few months.*

Occasionally it would rattle the windows, to warn you against venturing out. Or shake the tops of the trees at you like a fist.

I had a bagful of homework to do, but I wasn't in the mood.

I looked out my window at Liv's house. Liv lives next door. I told you that already.

It would have been perfect if Liv's bedroom faced my house. But her parents weren't prepared to give up their double bedroom with walk-in robes and ensuite so that Liv and I could face each other in the mornings and wave hello.

Sometimes you had to wonder what the good of parents were.

I texted Liv. 'Hey.'

'Hey,' she texted back.

'Whatcha doing?'

'Yumi's over. We're doing homework.'

'Srsly?' I texted.

'Where's my sarcastic-face emoji. Must invent one. No. As if. Come over.'

Liv's bedroom has a museum-type quality to it: there are butterflies and bugs pinned in ruler-straight lines all along her walls, twenty, maybe thirty of them, the common and Latin name written under each. She also has an old cabinet that belonged to her grandma with shallow, flat drawers that pull out to reveal yet more neatly arranged butterflies.

Lately, she'd been going to a pest-control place and buying even more bugs – bags of bugs for twenty bucks a pop. A lot of them had been crushed or damaged from the extermination process, but there were usually a few perfect ones Liv could use from each bag, for her art folio. First she sketched gigantic fine-ink drawings of them; then she carefully pinned multiple real teeny bugs on top of the sketches, giving them a sort of weird, 3D, crawling, buggy feel.

But while the top half of Liv's bedroom is geometric-precise – her pinned bugs, her intricate sketches painstakingly crafted – the bottom half is always a disaster zone.

'Don't get me wrong,' I said to her as I noticed my denim skirt on her floor, where it lay among the T-shirts, skirts, shoes, boots, bags, wet towels, cups and plates all left where they'd fallen, 'I also don't see the point in putting things in the wardrobe only to take them back out and put them back on, but when the clothes are actually mine, I think it would be reasonable to not dump them on your floor.'

'And you came over why?' Liv said. 'Remind me.'

'Hey, omigod,' Yumi interjected, holding up a cute little bag. 'Mine!'

Liv looked from one to other of us with sarcastic eyes. That's the only way I can describe them – sarcastic eyes. Like everything that was about to come out of her mouth was going to be heavily sarcastic and we'd better be ready for it.

'Here I am,' she said, 'leaving all your things out on my floor to remind you to take them back, making my room all messy in self-sacrifice, being a most excellent friend, and this is the thanks I get: a whole lot of criticism. A whole lot of blah blah blah.'

'That's mine too,' Yumi said, picking up a jumper that was hanging off the back of Liv's door. 'I forgot you had that.'

'Feel free to thank me whenever,' Liv said.

'Thank you?' I said. 'We should be arresting you.'

Liv shook her head sadly. 'You see,' she said, 'that's why I shouldn't be friends with you anymore.'

I felt myself wincing as if pinched, and saw (but maybe I was wrong) a slight pulling-in of Liv's mouth as she realised too late what she'd said.

It had been six weeks now, and Anouk still hadn't uttered a word in my general direction. Not a word. Friendship. Over.

And – not that I wanted to dwell – Jed had been all over Facebook, Insta, Snapchat, without throwing me a single bone. Nothing. Not a poke, a like, a comment, a chat, a text, a this, a that, a whatever. Complete radio silence.

Not a bone from Jed. Not a word from Anouk.

There was a new royal family featuring on the covers of *New Idea* and *Woman's Day*: Jed, King of All Bastards, and Anouk, Queen of the Grudge. As it had turned out, they would have been the perfect couple after all.

Yesterday, at lunchtime, I'd asked if anyone wanted a Twistie, offered the pack around (I was eating a lot of shit, because, well, why wouldn't I – who cared?), and when I'd passed it in Anouk's direction, she'd stared straight ahead as if I were invisible, her cheeks sucked in with pissed-off-ness.

Bitch.

I'd stopped complaining about her to Liv on the tram-ride home each afternoon from school, but only because when I bitched about her it made Liv go all monosyllabic on me, and Liv's normally way too opinionated for one-word answers. Plus, it was grotesquely boring – listening to myself, even I felt bored; I'd heard it all before, a million times over the past weeks. There was nothing new to add. So now I said nothing, and a little sliver of awkwardness had wedged itself between me and Liv.

Between me and Yumi, too. Yumi was like Switzerland – neutral. Whenever I complained about Anouk, she'd go all 'hmm', and it bugged me that she didn't say instead, *Yeah, she's a class-A bitch*. Sometimes I even had the unsettling feeling that she thought I was being slightly unreasonable but didn't want to say anything because she didn't want to hurt my feelings.

I hated Anouk for the monosyllables. And for Switzerland.

So when Liv said, that day in her bedroom, *You see, that's why I shouldn't be friends with you anymore*, it had felt a lot more pointy and sharp than it would have before Jed's party.

I picked up a pair of hoop earrings that I hadn't even realised were missing and said, 'These are mine too.'

Not that I cared about the earrings. But I wanted to put a new sentence into the air, to take over from the one that was hanging over all our heads.

'Exactly,' Liv said, implicitly agreeing with me to pretend not to notice the weirdness. 'I'm exactly awesome for leaving all your stuff out.' And she picked up her phone and started scrolling through whatever, as she waited for us to thank her for her human kindness.

Then she said, 'Ooh,' almost a gasp, like she hadn't meant to make a noise, and put her phone down again. Yumi and I both looked over at her.

'What?' Yumi said.

'Nothing,' Liv said.

'You can't "ooh" and then not tell us,' I said, grabbing her phone and tapping her password in, but not getting all the numbers out because Liv had grabbed it back from me.

I stared at her.

I wasn't her parent. She didn't have secrets from me.

I picked up my own phone and started scrolling through my feed to see what she'd oohed about. But there was nothing there. Then I heard a small intake of breath from Yumi, over at her phone. Whatever it was, Liv and Yumi both had it, but it hadn't come through to me.

I looked from Liv to Yumi, then back to Liv. 'What is it?' I asked.

Even though I wasn't sure I wanted to hear it.

Liv shook her head as if she didn't want to say – or maybe as if it wasn't really that big a deal. Then, realising she pretty much had to show me, she held her phone up, screen facing me, waving it so that my eyes couldn't get a good grip on it at first, and she said, 'It's ... um ... just Anouk sent through a thing, that her mum's away in a few weeks' time and she's going to have a ... some people over.'

I felt my mouth filling with Anoukness, my eyes pricking with tears.

'Awesome,' I said, sarcasm front and centre. 'Par-tay!'

'Hardly a party,' Liv said.

'You'll be invited, MC,' Yumi said at the same time, putting her phone face-down on the bed. 'For sure. Won't she, Liv? Anouk's probably forgotten she's blocked you. She probably thinks, right this moment, that you've got your invite.'

'Definitely,' Liv said. 'You'll definitely be invited. There's no way you wouldn't be.'

And that, right there, felt like one of the saddest things that had ever happened to me.

Liv only ever had three modes: rude, sarcastic or smart-arse.

Out of everything, I didn't think I could bear it if Liv turned all supportive on me.

Chapter 9

I didn't stay at Liv's. I didn't want to be there with her and Yumi and the invite from Anouk on two out of three phones. So I said homework called and went back home.

I had never made excuses to leave my friends before. Add that to the list of things I hated Anouk for.

I sat back down at my desk and looked out my window, over towards Liv's house, where her and Yumi were probably talking about the party. The sky was grey, but the wind had dropped, like it was trying not to annoy me now that I hadn't been invited to Anouk's.

My textbooks were open in front of me, I was logged on to the school portal, but every word was floating off the page and screen, unable to be pinned down.

Mum came to my door. 'I've had the best idea ever,' she said, leaning against the doorframe.

I turned to look at her. Best Idea Ever was exactly what I needed.

'I was thinking it might be nice,' Mum said, looking down at her fingernails, as if the world's smallest script was written on her cuticles, 'if we had a mother–daughter afternoon. I thought maybe I'd book us in to that place around the corner – you know, that place, what's it called ...' She looked away from her nails, up at the ceiling, out the window. 'Where you can get waxing and whatever ... Brazilian Butterfly. What do you think?'

I blinked at her.

'We can go there, get our bits zhooshed ...'

Bits?

Zhooshed?

'... and then maybe go see a movie, or get something to eat somewhere. An early dinner.'

I looked at her. Seriously, I didn't even know where to start.

So I started with, 'Ew.'

I hadn't meant it to sound so harsh, but it was an instinctive reaction. Of all the things I wanted to do that afternoon, of all the things that constituted Best Idea Ever, having a Brazilian with my mum wasn't one of them.

It was as if I had created a vacuum, the weather from outside rushing into my room. A coldness settled over Mum's mouth.

'Fine,' she said. 'That's fine. Perfect. I'll go on my own. You stay here. I can see that the thought of spending even a moment with me is too much for you to bear.'

'Bu—'

'Apparently,' she cut in, 'it's fine to have a girls' day with your father's new girlfriend and get your nails done, and Thai takeaway, and help them set up their new house, but not so much when it's spending time with your own mother.'

Her voice broke on 'own mother', and she left my room abruptly.

'Probably because she wasn't trying to bond over our vaginas,' I said through the open doorway. Not loudly enough for her to hear, of course.

She came back into my room.

'*MC*,' she spat, true fury in her voice, 'I was not trying to *bond* with you over our *vaginas*.' Okay. So apparently I hadn't said it as quietly as I'd thought. 'I simply wanted to try to have a nice day with you. None of this is what I wanted for my life. I'm trying to make the best of things, and you spend most of the time looking at me like I'm chopped liver. Well, here's a newsflash for you – I've had enough. I've had it up to here with your attitude.'

She chopped at her hairline with the blade of her hand to show exactly what level she'd had it up to.

My mouth dropped open. She'd had enough?

'You've had enough?' I said. '*You've had enough?*' I yelled. 'Well, newsflash right back at you – Guess what? He's my dad too. I lost him as well. He didn't just leave you; he left me too. And Harley. You think it's all about you. Well, it's not. You're the grown-up here, and your best suggestion is a mother–daughter *Brazilian*? I mean, seriously, what planet are you on? Just ...'

I wavered. I wanted to yell at her to fuck off. I was knife-edge close to unleashing exactly those words. I'd wanted Best Idea Ever. She'd promised me Best Idea Ever, and she'd fallen so far short, she'd probably broken some kind of Olympic record.

'What?' she said, her hand at her mouth. As if she regretted, maybe, all the words that had come out. Including her Best Idea Ever.

But I didn't answer. Instead, I stood up from my desk, kicked my chair away from me, not caring that it skittered across the floor and bashed into the wall, and then pushed my way out of my room, stumbling on all the broken words that lay on the floor between us, and slammed into the bathroom, where I could lock the door and not be busted in on.

Where the sound of my crying could be muffled by the running water of the shower that I stood in for a good half an hour.

By the time I came back out of the bathroom, I could hear the emptiness of the house, as if everything 'family' had drained away down the plughole.

Harley came out of his bedroom. He looked across at me. 'Hey,' he said.

Not *whatcha doing*. Not *let's go do something*. Just hey.

Then he went downstairs, without saying another word.

Chapter 10

It was, I'd realised after a sleepless Saturday night, like Anouk had stumbled upon the most sophisticated divide-and-conquer plan ever devised.

By having a party and not inviting me, she had turned that sliver of a wedge between Yumi and Liv and me into a gigantic keystone – heavy as a rock and awkward to clamber over. I wasn't sure she could have planned for it to go as well as it had for her.

On one side of the wedge was Anouk's party. On the other side was me.

So, I came up with a plan.

Admittedly, it wasn't a great plan. It sounded good when it spiralled crazily into a fully formed idea inside my head that afternoon. But once I put it out into the universe that Sunday night, it started looking less like a good idea and more like the stupidest thing I'd ever done.

I sent out a rival invite. Opened my computer, went on Facebook, and asked everyone to come to my house the night of Anouk's party.

'Mum's going out,' I posted. She wasn't. I'd sort that out later. 'In three weeks' time. On the 18th. Party. My house. Who's in?'

Okay. I get it. Gimpy doesn't even come close to describing it.

No one replied.

A couple of hours later I took it down.

The next morning at school, it was like all my friends and I had agreed, without anyone saying an actual word, that we'd all pretend no one had seen it. Liv talked about the biology assignment she hadn't finished over the weekend. Yumi complained about Wilder forcing her to watch some movie she hadn't liked about some kid on a bicycle. Hattie showed the impressive black eye she'd got from the other team's elbow, and complained about how basketball was supposed to be a non-contact sport.

The invitation I'd sent out wasn't mentioned. By anyone.

Actually, that's not true. One person mentioned it. Anouk.

She walked past me at the lockers after maths and said, 'Heard you're having a party on the eighteenth. I won't be able to make it, I'm afraid, because a bunch of people are coming over to mine. But it sounds like it's gonna be huge. I so wish I could be there. Anyway. See ya. Wouldn't wanna be ya.'

And she waggled her fingers at me in a trilling wave and walked off, a splutter of laughter coming out of her mouth. They were the first words she'd spoken to me in over six weeks, and she'd used them to insult me.

You've heard the expression 'seeing red'? I never fully understood it until that moment. The entire world around me shaded over, as if 3D glasses with red lenses had been fitted over my eyes, shifting the focus of everything a fraction.

Except instead of everything jumping into focus, the opposite effect was true: everything went out of focus. Blurry. Tipping.

I turned away from my locker, didn't even shut the door, and started walking, then running, down the corridor, away from everyone, away from class, biting on my mouth to keep it closed, as if vomit was about to come out of it and I needed to reach the toilet before it splattered on the floor at my feet.

But it wasn't vomit that was building up inside my mouth.

I ran down the stairs, across the quadrangle, over to the farthest corner of the oval.

And that was when it came out: a flaming-red – no, technicolour – fiery, furious, punch-a-hole-in-the-wall scream. No words, just pure sound, my body doubled over, my fists clenched, my eyes squeezed almost inside-out, my mouth as wide as it could go. A torrent of noise from deep down inside of me, hurled out.

Warning the world that I was mad as hell.

And there was a fair chance I wasn't going to take it anymore.

♡ ◯ ↱

Three weeks later

17th June

My life as a lettuce

Chapter 11

The night before Anouk's party, Liv and I were over at Yumi's.

'Seriously, it's pretty shit that she's not inviting you,' Liv said, her feet up on my lap. 'I get that she's annoyed, but hello, let go of the grudge. Plus, obviously we won't go if you're not invited but, I mean, there are so many people going, and she's just making it that we're all going to have to miss out because she's having a sook.'

'Definitely,' Yumi said from her spot on the floor, her fingers crawling like spiders along the spines of vinyl, searching for the exact right thing to play.

'We should call the police,' I said. 'Tomorrow night. Complain about the noise. Get them to shut it down early. It'd serve her right.'

Liv flicked a look over at Yumi, and then flicked back to me.

'I mean, obviously we wouldn't really call the police,' I added. 'I'm just saying it would be kind of funny.'

Of course, I definitely was saying we definitely should call the police. Why not? Anouk deserved it. She was going out of her way to make my life shit. It was only fair that I paid her back. It would give us a little something to look forward to tomorrow night at my house.

Yumi took out the all-white cover of the Beatles' *White Album* and slid the record from its sleeve.

Liv scrolled through her newsfeed, the whorl on the top of her freshly shorn head visible as her face tilted down towards her phone.

'But yeah, I mean, I'm just joking about calling the police,' I said again.

Feel free, either of you, to say you think it's actually a good idea.

'It would be a dog act if we did,' I added. Clearly it didn't sound as good an idea outside my head as it sounded inside. I sighed. 'What's Emile doing?' I asked Yumi, watching her gently lift the needle and place it carefully into the black groove. 'He should come round to mine too. We can still have a good night. I mean, not huge, obviously, but still.'

'Oh,' Yumi said, sitting back on her heels and looking at me as 'Back in the USSR' fired up. 'I think ... he's going ... to Anouk's. I mean, yeah, he said he was going. Because, like, quite a few of those other guys will be there, so yeah, I think he thought he might go.'

I looked from Yumi to Liv.

'But I'm not,' Yumi added. 'I mean, Emile can go. I don't care. But I've already told him I'm going to hang with you.'

'Party at yours,' Liv said, but it seemed like there was maybe a tinge of sarcasm to it.

'Yeah, well, personally,' I said, 'I think it's ridiculous. And totally low. The only reason she's probably having a party is so that she can specifically not invite me. I would never do that to her. I wouldn't do it to anyone. And the annoying thing is, it means you guys miss out too, because obviously she knows you wouldn't go if I don't go. So it's kind of like she hasn't invited the three of us. Like you said before, Liv.'

'Hang on a sec,' Liv said abruptly, putting her phone down and looking me bang in the eye. 'I've just had the best idea. You should come. Come with us. We'll all go. What's she going to do? Kick you out? She won't kick you out if you're with us. She's being a douche. Just crash with us. It'll be fine.'

'That's brilliant,' Yumi added. 'Even just for a couple of hours. And as soon as you want to leave, we'll come too.'

'I ... There's no way,' I said, slowly shaking my head. 'God, imagine how she'd be if I rocked up. She went psycho that day in English. She'd go completely nuts.'

'There are going to be so many people – she wouldn't even know you were there,' Yumi said.

'Exactly,' Liv said, as if it was settled. 'It's the perfect plan.'

I looked at Liv. She picked at her fingernails.

I slid my eyes over to Yumi. She started running her fingers along the spines of her vinyl again.

'I think she'd know if I was there,' I said to them. And as I said it, I realised: There was a massive party. And they wanted to go.

I felt my mouth fill with tears, a precursor to them washing out my eyes. I looked down at Liv's feet plonked on my knees, her toes pointing towards the ceiling.

'You know what?' I said, swallowing the tears back down my throat. 'I mean, if Emile's going, and everyone's gonna be there, you guys should go.'

I lifted Liv's feet off my lap, slowly, so she wouldn't think I was upset – it seemed important that neither of them picked that I was upset – and stood up.

'No,' Yumi said, her smudged freckle making her look even more tearful than normal. 'There's no way I'm going. I mean, it's definitely pretty bad that she isn't inviting you. But we'll stay with you.'

'I just have to go to the toilet,' I said and walked out of Yumi's bedroom into the bathroom. Shut the door. Locked it. Looked at my face in the mirror, my chin crumpling, my eyes welling, my forehead shattering into tiny pieces.

They wanted to go to Anouk's party. Of course they wanted to go.

But I wanted them to stay with me. They were my best friends. They were supposed to stay with me. I was going to have the worst night of my life, and they should be there for it.

That was what friends did for each other.

I turned on the tap and splashed my face, trying to staunch the tears coming from inside me by flooding my eyes with water from the outside.

It wasn't fair. And now, I realised, I couldn't even vent to Yumi and Liv about it. Meaning the wedge of Anouk's party had now fully separated us. We weren't us, the three of us, anymore. Instead, we were me, and them.

Fook Anouk.

I wanted to get out of there, away from them, but I couldn't just leave, because then it would seem like I was upset. Now that we were on opposite sides of the wedge, I definitely didn't want them to see me crying.

I texted Mum. 'Can you come get me from Yumi's?'

'Everything okay?' popped back almost immediately on her side of text screen.

'Just don't feel well. Text when you're out front.'

'Lucky timing. I'm coming back from the supermarket. I'll be there in 5.'

I went back into Yumi's bedroom. 'I just got a text from my mum,' I said, holding up my phone as if proof were required. 'She said she's got some things she needs to do with me, so she's gonna swing by and pick me up. Like, now.'

'Oh,' Yumi said. 'Are you okay?'

'Yeah. For sure.'

'We're not going to Anouk's party unless you come,' Liv said.

'It won't be any fun without you,' Yumi said.

I shook my head. 'It's fine. You should go. I really don't want to. Anyway, I think I'm getting a cold,' I said, putting my hands up to my throat.

'Oh,' Yumi said. 'Right. I think a few people have been sick lately.'

'Even if we did go,' Liv said, sounding exactly like a person who was planning on going, 'we'd only go for a little while. It won't be that good. You won't be missing out on anything.'

I nodded.

'MC, do you really think we should go?' Yumi said, slathering on the insincerity.

'If you want us not to go,' Liv said, slapping on more insincerity, 'we definitely won't. But I totally get that if you're not feeling good, you probably want to stay home. And if you're going to do that, I guess then we might as well go. It's not like you'll want us hanging over at yours, if you're not feeling good.'

I looked from Liv to Yumi, then back to Liv. I wasn't sure I'd be able to get any words past the lump that was damming up my throat.

'Oh, for sure,' I said. 'You definitely should go. Uh … I think my mum's here.' I looked down at my phone, then walked out of Yumi's bedroom.

No hugs goodbye. No kisses. Just me, my mouth a grim line, my arms folded across my chest, alone on my side of the wedge.

When I got to the bottom of the stairs I saw that Mum actually was standing at the front door, talking to Yumi's dad.

What parent came inside the house for a pick-up? I needed to get to the car. I wasn't sure I was going to be able to keep it together much longer.

'See ya, Mr Yumi,' I said.

Not Mr Martin. I hadn't been able to stay mad at him. Of course I hadn't. How could you stay mad with Mr Yumi?

'I was just telling your mum,' Mr Yumi said, stopping me mid-stride with a gentle arm barricading my way, 'that I feel like things have been a bit unsettled for you lately. At school.'

'Well,' Mum said to Mr Yumi, 'you know Dennis and I have split up. And now he's moved into a new place, and he's got a new girlfriend.'

'It's nothing to do with Dad,' I said, my voice shaky. 'I'm fine. Everything's fine.'

'I've noticed some tension between you and Anouk,' said Mr Yumi, Master of the Understatement.

'It certainly has been a difficult time for the family. For all of us. I'm not surprised she's feeling unsettled,' Mum said.

I narrowed my eyes at her. Slit my mouth. Mr Yumi didn't need to know any of this. 'Let's go,' I said, grabbing her arm.

'Well, yes, I understand it's a tough time for all of you,' Mr Yumi said. 'But it's the friendship thing that has me worried. For example, the girls mentioned a party at Anouk's tomorrow night, and I wanted to check if . . .' Then he looked at me; looked over at Mum.

The girls had *mentioned* a party? That meant Yumi had already checked with him that she could go, even though she'd been telling me all this time that she was totally going to hang out with me the night of the party. It hadn't been long ago that I would have trusted Yumi and Liv with every single thing in my life. And now . . . well, now I had to hear what was actually going on from Mr Yumi.

I tuned back in. '. . . and without Dennis to back me up,' Mum was saying, 'it's just impossible for me to get her to listen. That's why I think you're so wonderful with Yumi and Wilder. You've been doing the single-parent business for a while now. Maybe I need to sit down with you and get a few pointers. You know, a glass of wine? You could come for dinner one night?'

I felt my throat thickening. Was she flirting with Mr Yumi?

Mr Yumi smiled at her, then at me. 'That's very kind of you, Julie,' he said, 'but I'm usually pretty busy, with work. And the kids.'

'Oh, of course,' she said, shaking her head as if he'd got it all wrong – as if there was no way Mrs Tinder here would ever hit on Mr Yumi. 'I just meant a barbecue and salad or something. With the kids. Simple, easy. That's all.'

I couldn't believe she was actually flirting with him. She'd known Yumi's mum. They'd been friends.

If my friendship with Yumi wasn't completely dead and buried, it would be if Mum made any serious moves on Mr Yumi.

I shouldered past Mum, knocking into her, and started walking towards the street. Yelled, 'I'll be in the car,' over my shoulder – loudly.

I sat in the front seat, trying to settle my breathing, my chest pounding as if my heart were being held prisoner in there behind the bars of my ribs.

So, my friends had always planned on going to the party, and Mum was making a serious play for Mr Yumi. My life was shit, and I felt like I had less and less room to move. Certainly fewer and fewer people to vent to.

In fact, make that *no* people left to vent to. I couldn't tell anyone how I felt. No one.

Inside, the pounding against my ribs grew louder.

I was all I had left.

Chapter 12

The day of Anouk's party, the air had a freeze through it, like someone had closed the door on the worldwide fridge and we were all living our lives on its shelves.

I felt as popular as limp lettuce.

I didn't see anyone. Didn't go round to Liv's, didn't see Yumi, didn't reply to their texts. Everyone was getting ready to go to Anouk's that night, and I couldn't bear listening to them get excited about it – or not-talk about it because they didn't want to hurt my feelings.

I hated Anouk.

Mum always says you shouldn't say you hate anyone. But Mum was wrong – you should hate someone if they made you hate them.

In fact, 'hate' was too kind, too sweet, a word; it didn't properly capture the level of venom that I was feeling towards her. My shoulders had risen up to bracket my face, as if trying to physically block the sound of any Anoukness from reaching my ears. There was a dry, brittle Anouk-lump in my chest. I couldn't eat because of all the Anoukness churning in my stomach.

Yeah, 'hate' didn't even come close.

I kept scrolling through my phone, looking through everyone's feeds to see what they were doing. Hattie was over at Anouk's. Liv was at Yumi's. Everyone I knew, pretty much, was getting together, getting geared up to go to Anouk's massive party.

And me. I was at home. A lettuce.

#

That afternoon, Mum and Prue and Maude barged into my bedroom.

'Oh,' Mum said, stopping short when she saw me in my bed, Prue and Maude walking into her back like they were part of a cliched seventies comedy sitcom: *ba-doiiinnngg*, laugh-track, exaggerated expressions. 'What are you doing here, MC? I thought you were at Yumi's.'

'No,' I said. 'I'm here. In bed. Obviously.'

'You're not going to that party tonight?' Prue asked me, looking confused.

Relief lapped at my chest. The fact that Prue hadn't expected to see me at home meant Liv hadn't told her anything. Which was good. Mr Yumi saw us at school every day; he'd watched the dynamics shift. It wasn't *that* surprising that he was onto the situation. But if I'd thought Liv had sat down at her kitchen table and said to her mum, *I'm worried*

about MC and Anouk; not sure how I should handle it. MC's
not invited to Anouk's party. How should I play it? I didn't think
I could have dealt with it.

Besides, you know, parents – they're always trying to step
in and fix things, as if we're not capable of sorting stuff out
ourselves.

Yeah, parents, guess what, we can.

'I've got a cold,' I said.

Mum came over and put her hand on my forehead. 'You're
not going to Anouk's?' she checked.

I shook my head.

'Is everything alright?' she said to me, softly, like it was just
between me and her. 'When Yumi's dad said yesterday …'

'I'm fine,' I said, pushing her hand away. 'I've got a cold,
that's all. I've got a headache. I don't feel like going to a party
tonight. So sue me.'

She put her hand under my chin, thumb one side of my
neck, fingers the other side.

'Your glands aren't up,' she said.

I pushed her away again. 'I just don't feel good. Anyway,
what are you all doing in my room?' I said, swinging the
spotlight away from me and back over to them – because hell,
what *were* they all doing in my room, barging in like they'd
thought I'd never catch them?

'Well,' Mum said, looking slightly embarrassed, 'the thing
is, we didn't know you were home.' Yeah, I'd figured that part
out for myself. Then she put the back of her hand to the front
of my wardrobe, like she was trying to sell it to me, and said,
'And … uhhh … I'm going out tonight.'

'Girls' night,' Maude added quickly.

'And … I thought maybe I might have a look at what you've got in here,' Mum said, opening my wardrobe door, 'because all my clothes are old. I need a revamp. My shoes have heels on them that haven't been seen since the eighties. And I remembered those shoes I bought you last year for your formal – remember those? I don't think you even ended up wearing them …'

She leant over and pulled out a shoebox and, yes, she was right, I'd never worn them because, well, if you could see them, you'd know exactly why I'd never worn them.

'… and I thought they might go with the dress I was thinking of wearing tonight.'

She flipped the shoebox lid in a tada moment and showed the contents to Prue and Maude.

'They're perfect,' Prue said, pulling one of the shoes out of the box and holding it up to examine it.

'You think?' Mum said.

'Take them,' I said. 'Consider them sold, to the highest bidder.'

'A couple of those necklaces might be nice, too,' Maude added, unhooking some sparkly strands off their nail on my wall.

'Whatever,' I said and burrowed my head under my doona.

Because when you're feeling unpopular and unloved, it's great to know your own mother has a better social life than you do.

#

Mum left money on the kitchen bench for a pizza, but even lifting the phone seemed like too much contact with the outside world; too much of an admission of what a loser I was.

Even just to the pizza guy.

Instead, I went through the cupboards to see if I could find anything to eat. There was an opened bag of spiral pasta with not much in it, a handful at most, although once it was cooked it would expand and probably be enough for a meal for one.

Add a tin of tuna.

Grate some cheese.

Pasta, tuna and cheese. One of my favourite meals.

I plugged my phone into the stereo and put Hockey Dad on, cranked up loud and proud. Maybe the night wasn't going to be as bad as I'd thought it would be. I'd have some spiral pasta, watch a movie, avoid social media, make my own fun.

In fact, I didn't even care that I wasn't going to Anouk's stupid party. And there was a pretty good chance that I'd call the cops and put in an official noise complaint, because why wouldn't I, and yeah, she was a bitch but I didn't care because I had the entire house to myself, and there was always something good about that.

I was dancing round the kitchen to 'I Need a Woman' when I heard a knock on the door.

I stopped dancing, as if I'd been sprung.

If Mum or Harley had have been home, I'd have left it for them, but it was just me, on my own, and I couldn't not answer it because the stupid music was playing.

Stupid Hockey Dad.

I opened the door. Standing there were a couple of girls from school, and some guys I knew, friends of Jed's.

Not great friends of mine. Kind-of friends. People I knew. Not people I wanted to have coming to my house on the night when I was missing out on the biggest party of the year.

I stared at them. 'Hi,' I said, and frowned.

'Hey,' one of the girls, Nique, said, holding up her backpack, the clink of bottles coming from inside. 'We thought we'd come here, have a couple of drinks. Then go with you guys to Anouk's.'

I felt like I was suddenly in a whole different dimension or something. A place where I was invited to Anouk's, and friends were turning up at mine to have pre-drinks beforehand.

But I wasn't in a whole different dimension. I was here. In Melbourne. Right now. 'What are you talking about?' I asked.

'You know,' Nique said, uncertainty starting to fog her face, mirroring the cottony confusion I was feeling inside my own head, 'you put that thing on Facebook a couple of weeks ago, saying you were having a party tonight? I mean, obviously not a full party, seeing as Anouk's is on, but yeah, you know, remember, a couple of weeks ago? So we thought we'd come here, and have a couple of drinks with everyone' – she leant in through the doorway to see my house; to see the party of exactly zero – well, one if you included me – 'and then go with, um, you guys to Anouk's. Ah ... did I get something wrong? That thing you posted? You know. And

Della and Audrey and a few others said they were going to come round here before Anouk's too. But I don't know, has everyone ...'

And she didn't even finish her sentence, because her brain was farting with the effort of understanding exactly what was going on.

I looked at her.

I was having spiral pasta and tuna and cheese for dinner. There wasn't even a full bag of pasta; it probably wouldn't even fill a small bowl. And here they were, turning up, their backpacks full of booze. And here was me, the only person any of us knew who wasn't going to Anouk's party. One of them, Jack, even had the gall to be one of Jed's good friends, the fucker.

I looked at them, the smug lot of them, and said ... okay, maybe I shouldn't have done this, maybe I should have said that I was sick and left it at that, but I looked at the five of them with their smug, going-to-a-party faces and I said, 'I'm not going to Anouk's because she's a fucking bitch. Hope you have a shit night.'

And I slammed the door in their stupid faces.

Harley came into the kitchen through the back door.

'There's a bunch of people standing out the front,' he said.

I stared at him. Felt nothing – blankness.

It was so many months since I'd had any kind of proper conversation with Harley, I didn't even remember how to do it. And I didn't care anymore. I didn't care that things were weird with us.

I didn't care that ten minutes ago I'd yelled at Nique and all those guys to have a shit night.

I was a void.

A void.

Someone to avoid.

'One of them said to me,' Harley went on, talking even though I wasn't responding, '*The party isn't on.* Then when I said, *What party?* and that I live here, one of the chicks said, *Whoa. Good luck*, and said you lost it just before.'

I didn't move.

'Is everything okay?' he asked.

I blinked. I was a void no longer. 'Who's outside?' I asked him. 'How many people?'

'I don't know. Ten or something. Fifteen.'

'Tell them to fuck off.'

Harley looked at me, then walked out of the kitchen. I heard him open the front door, shout, 'Fuck off,' into the street, then shut the door and come back into the kitchen.

'Sorted,' he said.

I looked at him in a rush of wanting to cry, and then we both burst out laughing, the sort of gut-busting laugh that physically hurts all the way down your sides; laughter that organs weren't built to withstand; laughter as pain, as torture, which was exactly what I needed.

'That's so great,' I said, clutching my stomach to keep my body stitched together. 'You've told the entire world to fuck off on my behalf. I love it.'

'It was my pleasure,' he said, leaning back against the kitchen bench, a grin splitting his face.

'Omigod,' I said, putting my hand over my eyes, as if by not-seeing, I could make it not-real, 'I can't believe I just did that. What a dick. I seriously lost it. How embarrassing. And what if other people come over? I can't abuse everyone. I'd be exhausted by the end of the night.'

Harley laughed again. It felt good seeing a smile on his face. It had been so long.

'Let's go out,' I said to Harley suddenly. 'I don't want to stay here by myself tonight. And we haven't hung out for ages. Let's go see a movie or something.'

He hesitated. 'Where's Mum?'

'She's on a girls' night. Come on, let's go somewhere.'

I could hear the smallness in my voice. The need for my brother that I usually kept so well hidden these days.

'I can't,' Harley said. 'I would if I could, but I just dropped home to pick up some stuff. I'm meeting people in the city.'

'Oh, right.' I stepped back, out of his personal space. 'It's okay. Don't worry about it.'

Harley stepped forward. 'I would,' he said, putting his arm around my shoulders. 'I really would, but I'm meeting people. You want me to take you to ... what are Liv and Yumi doing?'

'They're at the party,' I said, 'that I'm not invited to.'

'Oh. Okay. Bummer. Well, how about I take you round to, I don't know, Grandpa's?'

You'd think he'd have suggested Dad first up, but Grandpa was as close as Harley got to referencing Dad these days.

'Yeah,' I said, the idea appealing to me as soon as it landed in my brain. Hang out with someone who thought I was amazing. Perfect idea. 'I'll give him a call and tell him I'm coming over.'

'Okay. I'll drop you round there on my way into the city,' Harley said, and he ran upstairs, taking them two at a time, to get whatever it was he'd come home for.

I called Grandpa's house.

It went through to his voicemail. I left a message, then called his mobile. No answer. Texted him. No answer.

Then again, he was a grandpa – he wasn't tethered to his phone like I was.

I called his home phone again. Still no answer. Then I remembered that Grandpa and his buddy Tony often went to the movies on a Saturday night, the two old friends – both of them wifeless – going to an early session, scoffing a glass of wine afterwards, then heading home to bed.

Even my grandpa had a better social life than me.

A message came up on my screen to say that Liv had just tried to call me – but my phone hadn't rung.

It was still doing that sometimes, going straight through to voicemail, for some reason. Texts had gone missing. The battery had been dying faster than it should have. It was driving me crazy.

I wondered, for the millionth time, whether maybe Jed had tried to call me a couple of times after his party, and when I hadn't called him back he'd thought I wasn't interested. Because otherwise it didn't make sense, him being so into me before we'd got together, and then afterwards, nothing.

Jed would be going to Anouk's party tonight, thinking that I'd be there. Maybe he was looking forward to seeing me. Maybe he was thinking that tonight, we'd hook up again.

I stared at my phone. Maybe I should text him. Just a quick little something, to say I wasn't going tonight, and seeing if maybe he wanted to hang out with me at my place, instead of going to Anouk's.

My screen lit up for a second time, reminding me that Liv had just left a message. I wondered whether she was at the party already, and if so, whether Nique had told her about my freak-out. I went into messages and saw that Liv had left a voicemail.

'Hey MC, just ringing to see if you're okay. You sure you don't want us to come round?'

I wasn't going to call her back. There was only so much insincerity a girl could stand – especially from someone who was supposed to be her best friend.

Harley came back into the kitchen, his car keys dangling off his pointer finger, a backpack dangling off his shoulder.

'You right to go?' he asked.

'Grandpa's not home,' I said, holding up my phone to face him, as if Grandpa's non-answer was written up there on the screen. 'And my phone's been weird lately – like, Liv tried to call just now, but it went straight through to voice message – and the thing is, there's this guy I like' – Harley raised an eyebrow – 'and I was with him, this guy, at a party a few weeks ago, but I haven't heard from him since, and I was thinking maybe it's because my phone's been messing up and he's tried to call me but I never got the message and now he thinks I'm not into him, but I am, at least I guess I think I am, and I'm wondering whether maybe I should text him and see if he wants to come round tonight and maybe he could hang with me here. What do you think?'

Harley looked away from me a moment, and then back.

'Well, first up,' he said, 'Mum might have put a tracking app on your phone. I found one on mine, so she could have done the same thing to yours.'

'What? WHAT? She's been spying on me? Are you joking?'

The prisoner that was my heart ran a tin mug back and forth against the bars of my chest, furious at yet another example of how shit everything in my life was.

'I'm just assuming,' he said. 'I don't know for sure.'

'Seeing everything I *do*? Everywhere I *go*?'

Harley looked at his watch, then put his bag down.

'It's easy enough to get off,' he said, taking out his phone and sending a quick text message to whoever he was meeting. 'We can fix it, if you want.'

I nodded, anger making my breath shorten into quick puffs.

'I can't believe she would do something like that,' I said as we walked together up the stairs to my bedroom. 'She's psycho. She's seriously lost it, since Dad moved out. What did she say when you told her you'd found a spy app on your phone?'

'She said she didn't know what I was talking about.'

'So does it mean she can read my emails, see all my text messages, see everything on my phone? I can't believe she would do that.'

Harley shook his head as he sat down at my desk and plugged my phone into my laptop. 'She can't see into your phone. She can just see where you are when you're out.'

Watching the icons pop up on the computer screen to show my phone was plugged in, I remembered a small thing from weeks ago – that day I'd gone into the city to meet Dad for lunch. Mum had asked me where I'd been after lunch. Like she'd known I'd gone somewhere else. To get a manicure.

Like she'd been spying on me.

'I still can't believe she would do this,' I said, shaking my head. 'We should put a spy app on her phone. See how she likes it.'

Harley laughed. 'What? And watch her go where?'

Tinder dates, for one, I wanted to say. But somehow it seemed mean to tell him. Like I'd be betraying Mum.

'I don't know,' I said. 'The supermarket?'

Harley laughed again and started backing up my phone onto the computer.

'So what about the other thing?' I said over his shoulder, the two of us facing my computer as the bar ran across the screen, backing up my photos, my music, my address book, everything. 'This guy? Do you think I should text him? Because maybe he tried to call me and I never called him back because Mum put a spy app on my phone and it hasn't been working properly and now I've hurt his feelings and that's why I haven't heard from him?'

Harley kept his eyes computer-side as he said, 'The thing is, if he tried to call and you didn't reply, he'd try again. Guys aren't put off that easy. Unless he's a real timid type. Is he timid?'

I thought about the carrot-fish trick; the dog-talking invitation; the way Jed had been straight onto the idea of going swimming with me and Anouk.

I sighed. 'No,' I said.

'Well,' Harley said, 'I hate to break it to you, sister, but he's just not that into you.'

'Thanks.'

'Just calling it as I see it.'

For someone who hadn't been doing much talking around the house these past few months, he really knew how to string a sentence together for maximum effect.

He's just not that into you. Right. Thanks for that.

Harley finished downloading all my stuff, factory-reset my phone, then downloaded all my stuff back onto it.

Then he turned around and looked at me.

'Sorry about the guy,' he said.

'I don't care,' I said. 'Doesn't matter.'

'Guys can be arseholes. You sure you're okay? I feel bad leaving you here on your own,' he said. 'Why don't you call Dad and see if you can go round to his place instead?'

It sounded strange, hearing the word 'Dad' coming out of Harley's mouth. Ever since Dad had moved out, Mum had only ever called him Your Father, and Harley hadn't bothered mentioning him at all.

It was nice to hear Dad's name. Like it was just an everyday thing.

So I called him.

I knew there was a chance, a good chance, a huge probability, that Tosca would be there with him. But sitting with the two of them was definitely a better option than sitting at home, perhaps hiding under the couch if anyone else knocked on the door.

'You there?' I asked when he answered. 'I thought I might come over.'

'Great. We'd love it.'

We.

Whatever.

#

Slowly, slowly, Dad was dropping the pretense of Tosca just happening to be there.

He had an apron tied around his waist as he opened the oven and took the frittata out. Tosca sat at the bench and chopped parsley and made a salad. Her hair corkscrewed all over the kitchen, like it was looking for a bottle of wine to open. A glass of wine sat on Dad's side of the bench, and a bottle of water on Tosca's side.

Welcome to domesticity, new-Dad style.

Dad talked about Brexit and America and blah blah blah who cares, and Tosca added bits and pieces about Australian politics and more blah blah who cares, and the two of them chatted like it was truly awesome to be at home sitting in the kitchen eating dinner together on a Saturday night.

I forked food into my mouth as I scrolled through Snapchat, clicking on all my oldest and most favourite friends' stories about the party I wasn't invited to.

Liv and Yumi with their arms around each other's shoulders, their heads tilted towards each other.

A photo Hattie had taken of Anouk in the middle of a bunch of people, her arms up, grinning at the camera, a flannelette shirt tied around her waist.

'I think you can put that away while we're having dinner,' Dad said.

I ignored him. Scrolled through more photos.

'MC,' he said.

I pushed the phone away from me. Not because he'd asked me to, but because I knew that going on social media was self-destructive and wallowing.

Then again, I was in the mood to wallow, so why shouldn't I?

Dad had Tosca; Mum had Maude and Prue – and Tinder; Harley was meeting people in the city; Grandpa was out; Liv and Yumi and everyone were at an enormous party.

I had no one.

I drew my phone back in towards me and started scrolling through more pics.

Eliza from the year above at school, sitting on the kitchen bench with Jed's friend Finn leaning in towards her.

Jed, looking handsome, standing out the back with Leo and Bronte and Jack and a couple of the other people who'd turned up at my place.

Nique and Harry and Charlie W in the hallway, cheers-ing the world with beers. Della and Audrey laughing their heads off.

'MC,' Dad said. 'I said to put that away.'

'I just need to look at this one thing,' I said, trying to find more shots of Jed. This wasn't a case of FOMO. This was a case of KIMO – Knowing I'd Missed Out.

Angus and Hugo and Henry and Charlie L, not even realising their photo was being taken as they talked about something intense. Probably footy.

Maddie and Bryce and Bianca and Holly, hugging in close to each other and grinning at the camera, looking vague and heavy-lidded as usual.

Tom and Greta and Pia and Charlie G and Will, all scrunched together to fit in the photo, Will's surfie hair giving him a just-off-the-wave look.

Emile with his arm around Yumi, looking like life couldn't get any better.

Hattie. Liv. Anouk. Yumi. Everyone. Laughing. Drinking. Hugging. Friends. Together.

Biggest party of the year.

'MC,' Dad said, 'that's it. While we're having dinner, I don't want your phone at the table.'

I glared at him, then pushed my phone away from me, sliding it over the bench too quickly. Dad reached out his hand and stopped it from toppling over the edge and smashing.

'Why, thank you,' he said, 'you're too kind,' and he pocketed it.

Because sarcasm – in case you're wondering – isn't dead.

#

Later that evening, the three of us were watching some boring movie from the eighties about vampires that Dad had – wrongly – told me I'd love while I scrolled through my phone again.

There weren't many stories being posted at this time of night.

There was too much fun being had for people to bother fishing their phones out of their pockets to take photos.

I went to the toilet, more for something to do than because I was really busting. You really know your Saturday night has hit an all-time low when going to the toilet is the highlight.

It was as I was washing my hands that I noticed something in the wastebasket – a box, with pink lettering saying 'Predict' running across the baby-blue background, standing right out among all the white tissues and cottonwool balls in the bin.

Predict.

I frowned and reached into the rubbish, picked out that pink-and-blue cardboard box.

I turned it over and read the writing on the back.

'This home pregnancy testing kit,' it said, 'works by detecting the presence of the hormone hCG (human chorionic gonadotropin) in a woman's urine. Known as the pregnancy hormone, hCG is only found in pregnant women. For instructions on how to use this kit, please read the instruction sheet inside.'

My heart stilled. My breathing stilled. Everything stilled. It was like the entire world had been switched to silent.

I'd been over here all night, and Dad hadn't even bothered to mention the little fact of a brand-new brother or sister to me.

I didn't want to be here.

I didn't want to stay the night anymore.

Not when the fact of brand-new baby wasn't being mentioned.

I went back out to the two of them. Tosca looked up at me from where she lay with her feet propped up on Dad's lap, and a look skittered across her face, like she'd just remembered she'd left the iron on or something. She got up and went into the kitchen. I heard her filling the kettle with water, putting it on the stovetop.

They were having a baby.

If someone had poked me at that moment – and I'm not talking Facebook here, I'm talking a little prod in my arm or my stomach or my back with their actual finger – I'd have crumbled like a shell of meringue, and everything would have come spilling out of the hole they'd just made in me.

I'd been sitting there all night, and they hadn't bothered to tell me.

'I just remembered,' I said to Dad, standing beside the couch, looking down at him, 'I have to get up early tomorrow morning. I have to go home …'

'But you said you'd stay,' he said, looking up at me, remaining on the couch. 'It's your first night in our new place.'

'Yeah, but I've got something on tomorrow, early, so yeah.'

'MC, just go from here. I can take you in the morning.'

'No, I've left stuff at home. I need to go home. Kind of now.'

He sighed. 'If I'd known you were going to get me to drive you, I wouldn't have had that second glass of wine.'

He didn't actually care that I was leaving; that I wasn't going to spend my first night in their house. He just didn't want to drive me home because he'd had two glasses of wine.

'Forget about it,' I said, feeling like the world was getting smaller and smaller, suffocating me. I just needed to get out of there. 'I'll catch the tram. I'll walk. I don't care. You stay where you are.'

'No, no,' he said, struggling to get off the couch like an old man, making a show of the fact he was having to get off his arse, 'I don't mind taking you; I just wouldn't have had that … doesn't matter, I've only had two glasses, I'll be fine, let me get my keys.'

'Tea?' Tosca called out from the kitchen.

'I'll have one when I get back,' Dad replied. 'MC's just remembered she's got this stuff she needs to do tomorrow.'

'Oh, okay,' Tosca said, coming into the hallway and leaning against the doorjamb, her arms folding in like a barrier over her stomach.

I eyeballed her. *Tell me*, I felt like saying. *Tell me*.

She looked away.

Dad grabbed his keys off the hallway table. 'Ready?' he asked.

I could feel tears threatening my eyes, but all I wanted was to get home with as little intervention as possible. If I started crying here in the hallway, Dad would be all blah blah what's wrong, and I didn't want to discuss it. He didn't want to tell me he was having a baby – fine. Then I certainly didn't want to start bubbling over with tears here in front of the two of them.

'I just have to go to the toilet,' I said.

'You just went.'

'Weak bladder,' I said, pushing the door shut behind me.

I looked at myself in the mirror. My cheeks were reddening in the corners, like my tear glands were set to explode with the pressure of the tears inside not being released. I ran cold water and splashed my face. It felt like I was doing that a lot this weekend. I put the towel against my face, dried the tears that had snuck out, settled myself down.

It was as I was putting the towel back on its rail that I noticed something. The tissues, the cottonwool balls, everything else in the rubbish bin was still the same. But the 'Predict'?

It was gone.

Tosca had removed it.

#

When we got out to the car, Dad opened the door for me.

'I can do that myself,' I said. 'I'm perfectly capable of opening my own car door.'

'I'm just being chivalrous,' he said, bowing down as he waved me into the seat with a flourish.

'Chivalry's sexist,' I said, grabbing the handle from the inside and slamming it shut myself.

See, perfectly capable.

Dad got into the car, put his keys in the ignition, and looked at me.

'Chivalry isn't sexist,' he said. 'It's not about strength or control or anything. It's about me being nice to you. You're barking up the wrong tree if you think chivalry's sexist.'

'Yeah? Well, you'd know,' I said. 'You'd know all about chivalry. Like, it's so chivalrous, to leave your wife and your kids and start shagging someone else.'

Dad's face stoned over.

'Don't you dare speak to me like that.'

'What? I'm just stating the obvious,' I said, my voice rising. And suddenly I made a decision. I opened the car door – all by myself, see that – and got out, then I leant back in so he wouldn't miss a word I was about to say. 'I don't want you driving me home. You've been drinking. I can get home myself.'

'MC, I've had two small glasses. Get in the car.'

'No. I'm not getting in the car. I'm walking home.'

'It's raining.'

'No. You know nothing that's going on in my life, and you don't even have the guts to tell me what's going on in yours. So you should go back inside and have another glass of wine, because I'm going home, and I don't need your help to get there.'

And I slammed the car door, really made sure it was closed, no doubt about it, then ran off down the street.

Rain tipped over me as I ran, like someone in the sky had a bucket and was targeting me specifically; the type of rain it was hard not to take personally.

At home, I opened the front door of our house and slammed it behind me.

My house. Not Dad and Tosca's house. Mine.

I was wet through, not just my skin, but all the way down to my bones.

A text dinged from Dad. 'Let me know you got home safe. I'll call you tomorrow. Sorry I opened the car door for you.' He'd ended it with a smiley face, as if we were all happy families.

I deleted his text with a stab of my finger. The rain pelted against the glass of the windows, like it was banging on the panes in sympathy. Or like it wanted me to come out and play some more. Thanks but no thanks, rain.

I listened to the underlying noise inside the house. The hum of the fridge. The quiet push of the central heating.

There was a stillness that told me I was alone.

I stomped upstairs into the bathroom, looked in the bathroom mirror, and suddenly felt completely drained. Mascara ran the length of my face, creating shadowy, sucked-in hollows. My skin was slick, and I looked wrecked.

Towelling myself off seemed too much like hard work, though, and what was the point anyway? I'd drip-dry eventually.

It was as that thought settled in my mind that a strange man came walking into the bathroom, pulling up short when he saw me.

Reports of the home invasions that had been happening recently around Melbourne flashed through my mind: families hiding in locked bathrooms or bedrooms while gangs rampaged in their homes, taking whatever they wanted — jewellery, computers, the car.

People being hospitalised if they confronted these guys.

I was home all alone. Mum was out with Maude and Prue. Harley was in the city somewhere. Even Liv wasn't next door, because she was at Anouk's.

I was completely on my own. Me and this man.

Fight or flight, I thought to myself.

Flight. Definitely flight. But I couldn't fly, because the man was standing in the doorway, blocking my only escape route.

I was going to have to go the fight option. All those years learning karate back when I was a kid flooded my brain. There was the punch-him-in-the-throat thing that would literally kill him if I pulled it off. Or the slide-foot-down-shin-onto-his-foot slam, to break a few bones.

I wasn't going down without doing some damage.

'Shit,' he said. 'Sorry. I thought we were here alone.'

Apologising. As if he'd broken into my house accidentally.

'You're MC, I guess,' he went on. 'I'm Jim.'

I blinked at him.

And then he held up one finger, like he was a teacher, and said, 'Question: where's the toilet?'

At that moment, Mum came up behind him. 'No, next door along.' She had her dressing-gown on, and her hands slid around his waist. Which was when she saw me – looked at me like I was not supposed to be here.

Don't worry, I felt like saying to her, *I feel exactly the same way.*

'You said you were staying at Dad's tonight,' she managed. 'You texted me.'

I looked from her to this guy, Jim.

'Omigod, Jesus,' I yelled at her, 'I thought you were a home invasion, God!' And I ran out of the bathroom and locked my bedroom door.

#

I stuffed my headphones into my ears.

I didn't want to hear a peep, not even a scrap, a whiff, a wafer, of Mum-and-that-guy-ness. I shook my head back and forth, figuring that any further images or thoughts or words or anything to do with Mum and him wouldn't be able to stick to the wall of my brain if I kept my head moving.

There was a *ding* from my phone. I looked at my screen to see a text message. From Anouk.

Let me repeat that for you one more time, in case you missed it: a text message from Anouk.

'Ha ha,' she'd written, and she'd attached a photo of Jed and some random girl, kissing in the kitchen, the party swirling around them. 'Looks like he doesn't want either of us.'

Then another text: 'Wish you were here,' with a kissy face.

Jed. And another girl. And Anouk, not even caring about Jed, about Jed and her, about Jed and the other girl – only caring about rubbing it in. To me.

Seriously.

Seri-fucking-ously.

There weren't even words.

Well, actually, there were words: fuck you, fook Anouk.

I read and re-read her text; stared at the photo of Jed and the girl.

Looks like he doesn't want either of us, she'd written.

Wish you were here.

Sure.

Liv needed to get cracking on creating that sarcastic emoji of hers, because Anouk could have done with it right there.

Jed. With some random.

I felt my heart chink, give a brittle crack, at the thought of how much space I'd given him inside my brain, while there he was, moved on to the next girl.

Not giving me a second's thought.

And Anouk. Loving the fact.

Looks like he doesn't want either of us. Wish you were here.

I hadn't thought she could make me feel any worse, but props to Anouk – she'd just made me sink lower.

I tried to think of something good to send back to her. Something great. Something that would shut her up. Cut her down.

And then I had my first idea.

I went onto that app, the talking-dog app, clicked the photo I still had of Jed's dog, and I recorded the word 'bitch' – just the one word – and I texted it to Anouk.

So it was like Jed's dog was calling Anouk a bitch.

But only because she was.

Anouk texted back, 'Ha ha!' with a winky face.

I looked at the text. She was completely fearless. She didn't give a shit. I could say what I liked to her, and she wouldn't give a flying fuck.

To think she'd used to be one of my best friends.

I should have been at that party. I should have been there with all my friends, cheers-ing the world in the hallway with Liv and Yumi, with Nique and Harry and Charlie; laughing with Della and Audrey.

Maybe standing in the kitchen kissing Jed.

But no one, none of my friends, were giving me a second thought. They weren't missing me. They weren't leaving early. They were all still there, having a good time.

I wanted to go round there, over to Anouk's house, and bail them all up, stand in the front yard and scream at them. Did they all think this was fine, that I wasn't there, that

I wasn't invited, that Jed was with this other chick? Did any of them even care?

Oh sure, MC, I thought, *that'd go down really well.* Everyone would think I was certifiable.

I wanted to yell out my window like a shaggy-headed girl from the seventies: *I'm mad as hell, and I'm not going to take this anymore.* Except it would just be me. Me yelling out the window into the storm, and no one else caring.

I wanted to vent on a grand scale, but the world wasn't interested.

I picked up my phone and looked at the photo of the Gun, still there on my screen. I pressed record again.

'Fuck you, Anouk, you fucking fucker.'

It felt good, the viciousness of the words suiting my mood.

I was going to text it to her, Insta it, Snapchat it; send it out to everyone I knew, so they could ... what? Think I was a psycho?

But I liked the way the Gun looked so furry-faced and serious as he swore at her. I liked my angry voice coming out of this calm-looking dog.

So I opened up my secret Tumblr account. And I uploaded the video of the Gun calling Anouk a fucking fucker, keying in below it: #GirlsAreBitches.

And then I had another idea.

This is the one I should have left alone.

I had hundreds of screen grabs on my phone of celebrities. Miley Cyrus, Liam Hemsworth, Troye Sivan, Kendall Jenner, Kylie Jenner, Rihanna, Taylor Swift, Justin Bieber.

I pulled all their photos into the talking-pet app, synced up the dots on their eyes and the lines on their mouths, then got each of them to give a spray to Anouk.

'What the fook, Anouk.'

'Fook you, Anouk.'

'Fook Anouk, go have a sook.'

I changed the speed setting on each one as I went, so that some sounded slow and deep, and others sounded high and chipmunky.

Sharing our private joke with the world.

Elle Fanning, Josh Hutcherson, Selena Gomez, Emma Watson, Jennifer Lawrence . . . Over and over again, variations of 'fook Anouk' Tumbling onto the internet.

#Rihanna

#ElleFanning

#ChrisPine

#MadAsHell

#Lol

#PartyBitch

#FookAnouk

Raging fury, consider yourself vented.

Chapter 13

The next morning when I woke up I kept my eyes closed and enjoyed a drowsy, behind-my-lids moment. A sense of calm lay over the top of me, keeping my doona weighted down comfortably.

I'd told the entire world that Anouk was a bitch. And the good thing was, none of my friends were ever going to know about it.

I picked up my phone. Opened agirlwalksintoaschool to re-watch some of my videos.

I was surprised to see a few people had re-blogged a couple of them, with comments like 'gotta download this app – this is brilliant' and 'hilarious' and 'best idea ever'.

For the first time in days, I actually cracked a genuine smile.

I went back over the videos. You'd have thought the Josh Hutcherson one might have been my favourite, or the Elle Fanning one, but actually the ones that made me laugh the most were Jon Snow saying, 'The whole reason we've built

that bloody great wall is to keep out all the fooking Anouks,'
and a painted portrait of the Queen in her tiara saying,
'Fook Anouk, go have a sook,' and, okay this one was pretty
weird and not even a celebrity, but a strawberry with a tiny
little mouth saying, 'You're a berry, berry, berry biiiiig bitch,
Anouk,' the voice speeded up so it sounded like a chipmunk.

There was something just the right kind of ridiculous
about those ones to make me laugh.

Because fook Anouk, go have a sook.

I texted Liv later that morning: Kristen Stewart mouthing my
words, 'Hey Liv, whatcha doing? Wanna hang out? Just you
and me, girl.'

Liv texted back. 'Ha ha! Come over,' she wrote, with a face
crying tears of laughter.

When I went up to her bedroom, she was sitting at her
desk in her pyjamas, short hair sticking up at the back, dregs
of mascara still on her lashes, marking up one of her insect
sketches – putting her eye to her microscope and checking
the detail on the bug she'd laid carefully out on the glass.

She turned around and grinned at me as I walked in.

'That's so great,' she said. 'How did you do that?'

'The Kristen thing?'

'Yeah.'

'It's this app. It's supposed to be to make dogs talk, but you
just put anyone's face on there and it works perfectly.'

'Show me,' she said, doing a gimme motion with her hands.

I was going to show her on my phone, but then I realised there were all the celebs bitching about Anouk on my version. So instead I picked up her phone and went onto the app store, pressed the little magnifying glass to search for the talking pets app and saw that I didn't need to bother – it was trending.

Liv downloaded it, then we both started screenshotting different celebs and making them talk for us – Emma Watson, Zac Efron, Justin Bieber; just whoever took our fancy, saying all sorts of things on our behalf – and posting them on Insta.

'MC is the absolute hottest chick ever,' I made Robert Pattinson say.

'I can only dream of being as completely and utterly cool as Liv Barrett,' Liv put in FKA Twigs's mouth.

And so it went – a mash-up of general adoring of us by every single celebrity we could think of.

As we screenshotted and posted, we avoided talking about Anouk's party. Both of us did. The two of us pretending like perhaps it just hadn't happened.

Until finally I couldn't bear it, and threw in like I'd only just remembered, screenshotting Gigi Hadid as I asked, seemingly completely carelessly, 'How was last night?'

Liv said, 'Last night?' like she wasn't exactly sure what I was referring to – like the party had completely slipped her mind – and then, 'Anouk's?' and then she shrugged and said, 'Yeah, it was fine. I mean, it was fun, but nothing special.'

I'd have preferred she'd said, *Yeah, the party was awesome, best party I've been to in ages, maybe in my entire life. Had a great time – great music, great night, great, great, great, so much*

great I can't even go through all the greats about it. How was your
boring Saturday night at home?

Because that's what the normal Liv would have said.

'Who was there?' I asked, wanting the detail, wanting to force her to say something I didn't want to hear.

'Um,' she said, looking away from me, back towards her bug drawing, pencilling in some detail, the celebrity-talking, the fun we'd been having, completely forgotten, 'the usuals. But I promise, it was nothing big. What about you? How was your night?'

'Oh yeah, my night was great,' I said, sarcasm making my words brittle. 'Tosca's pregnant, and Mum brought a guy home, who I thought was a home invasion, so yeah, great, great, just a normal, great Saturday night at home.'

'Whoa. Tosca's pregnant?'

'Apparently. I don't know. She might be. I don't care.'

I picked up my phone and opened the text Anouk had sent me.

'Anouk texted me last night,' I said, shoving the screen of my phone at Liv so she could see firsthand what a bitch Anouk was. 'And Jed was with this girl? And you weren't even going to tell me?'

I didn't care if Liv didn't want to listen to me vent. She was my ventee, it was the deal, it had always been the deal, and today I felt like venting.

'Sure, don't invite me to your party, Anouk, whatever,' I ploughed ahead. 'I don't care, but don't go out of your way to make me feel more shit about everything than I already do.'

Liv scrolled through Anouk's texts, the photo she'd sent of Jed, shaking her head.

'I can see why you might think it's bad that she sent these,' Liv said, 'but I think she was sending them as, like, "What the hell, why aren't you here, what are we fighting over this guy for?" type texts. I think she felt pretty bad that you weren't there.'

I snatched my phone back from Liv.

'"Wish you were here,"' I read out loud. 'Seriously, Liv, as if. If she'd wanted me there, she could have invited me.'

Liv bit down on her lip. 'But the thing is,' she said, 'I think Anouk did feel bad about not inviting you. Nique said she'd gone around to your house, and you kind of lost it, and I think that's when Anouk realised that it was actually really mean that she didn't invite you.'

'Oh,' I said, shaking my head in the hope that Liv's words couldn't enter my brain and get trapped in there, 'she only realised the *night of the party* that it was mean not to invite me? Seriously? I can't believe you're defending her.'

Liv sighed. 'I'm not defending her. But I hate that you guys are having this stupid fight over some stupid guy. I mean, Jed's an arsehole. Look at him.'

She took my phone and then presented it back to me, as if the proof was right there in the photo of him kissing Ms Random.

'He's always been an arsehole. I don't really get why so many girls like him, but, you know, I guess he's just not my type. But this whole thing with you and Anouk … it's just kind of shit. And I think she really does feel bad about you not being there. And you won't even believe her, because you're so mad at her. So what's this thing you sent through next?'

And she pressed the play button of the Gun saying, 'Bitch.'

She frowned at me and pressed play again. 'What's he saying?' she asked, bringing my phone closer to her face as if that would help her hear better. 'I can't quite get it. It sounds like a cough or something.'

It was muffled. Not terribly clear. And even though his mouth was moving open and shut, it wasn't specifically making the b-itch shape.

Which I was kind of relieved about.

It had seemed okay to send in a text to Anouk the night before, but sitting with Liv, imagining saying it to her with my own mouth, hearing it with my own ears, I realised how awful it would sound.

'It just says . . .' I fudged it. 'It's just like a woof sound. You know, because he's a dog.'

Lied? Yes.

Saved myself? Definitely.

Because if Liv couldn't hear it, here in her bedroom on a Sunday morning, Anouk would have had no chance at her party with all those people around.

Later that afternoon, I lay on my bed and rehashed my conversation with Liv. *I really do think she feels bad*, she'd said.

Liv was on Anouk's side. She didn't have my back anymore.

And Jed was with that other chick, and everyone at the party would have known about it, too.

Part of me wanted to unfriend him, but then it would look like I actually cared, and the only thing I had left in my life was the fact that maybe, just maybe, he didn't know I cared.

Maybe he didn't know that the whole reason Anouk and I were fighting was because of him.

No, who was I kidding? Of course he would have known.

And now with Liv backing Anouk, acting like Anouk had suddenly become the good guy in all of this, it—

Liv. Backing Anouk.

A strangled little sound came out of my throat, causing me to start.

And that was when I knew that I wouldn't be able to stand going to school the next day. Because I didn't feel mad as hell anymore. Instead, I just felt out-and-out sad as hell.

Chapter 14

The next morning, Monday, sure enough, I couldn't lift my head off my pillow. My arms felt heavy. My legs were like unattached logs.

I didn't want to face everyone, hear about Anouk's party, how awesome it had been. Or worse, have everyone stop talking as soon as I walked up.

I didn't want to turn up at school and have everyone look at me and think to themselves, *Jed hooked up with that chick – I wonder if MC knows.*

I didn't want to look at any of their faces, because whatever expression I saw there, I just knew it would make me feel worse.

'You're still feeling sick?' Mum said, taking the thermometer out of my mouth. 'It's probably lucky you didn't go that party on Saturday night, then.'

'Yeah.'

She put her hand on my forehead. It felt nice. Cool. I wanted her to leave it there.

We didn't hug anymore; didn't cuddle up on the couch to watch films on a Friday night like we'd used to when I was little. The most skin contact we had these days was if she gave me a cursory kiss on the cheek before I left to go out somewhere.

I kind of missed her.

'You don't have a fever,' she said, sitting back and looking at me, her eyes narrowing as if she was trying to pull me into focus. Something she hadn't done for months now. Not since Dad had moved out.

I could feel tears pushing against the backs of my eyes, but I held them in. 'I've got a really bad headache,' I said shakily, putting my hand up to my own forehead. 'I ... I think it's a migraine.'

I threw 'migraine' in because it sounded serious and I was pretty sure you didn't get a temperature with a migraine.

'You do look pale,' she said. 'But I'm working at the shop,' she went on. 'I feel bad leaving you here if you're not well.'

I snuggled back down under my doona. 'I'll be fine,' I said weakly, wondering if maybe I really did have a migraine, because I felt so shit. 'I just need to rest.'

'You sure?'

'Positive.'

She didn't move.

'I'm sorry that was all so awkward on Saturday night,' she finally said. 'When you got home from Dad's.'

I turned towards the wall. I really didn't want to talk about that; didn't want to have that particular picture in my mind any more than I had to.

'It's fine. I don't care.'

She lingered by my bedside.

'I don't care,' I repeated into the wall.

She leant over, kissed my cheek, barely brushing her lips against my skin, like usual, and walked out. 'I'll call you later to see how you're feeling.'

I heard her leave the house. Pulled my computer into bed with me and opened it up.

I went through my feeds, scrolling through everyone's posts of Anouk's party again: the drinking photos, the laughing photos, the me-not-there photos. 'Best night ever.' 'Still recovering.' 'Party hardy.' I knew I was wallowing, but there was something exactly right about doing this, about the hurt it caused me, seeing what a great time everyone had had, and how badly I'd missed out.

Liv had acted like Anouk was the good guy, all sad she hadn't invited me, but I knew that wasn't true. She would have had a fantastic time, with everyone round at her place, feeling popular. I wanted to prove it to myself, to point at her photos and posts and say to myself, *There, see – no regrets to be seen anywhere on that smug face of hers*, but I couldn't, because I was still blocked.

So I hacked her Facebook.

It was easy enough, seeing as 'qwerty' was my second attempt at her password and, yes, that was the one.

Let that be a lesson to you, Anouk. Try to have a little more imagination.

There were millions of photos, comments. I don't even need to go into what everyone had posted – you've been on Facebook after a party. You know what people post. And woven through all those photos was Anouk with her arm slung around people's shoulders, laughing, drinking, having a great time. Regrets? No. Sad I wasn't there? Didn't look like it.

My fingers started itching with comments I wanted to write – sarcastic, bitchy remarks, telling people to piss off. But then she'd know she'd been hacked. So instead, I poked every guy she knew (cute, bad, ugly, cool, uncool, anyone living and breathing) – retribution for the humiliation of Jed not poking me back.

I changed her language to Pirate English.

I liked every single ad that came up in her feed.

I felt like my own evil twin – my bitchy alter ego, screwing Anouk's Facebook page up. It was a good feeling.

I closed my computer, shoved it to the end of my bed and went down to the kitchen in my nightie. My teeth were unbrushed; ditto my hair. Which was when Harley came through the back door into the kitchen.

'Oh, hey,' Harley said, stopping short. 'What are you doing home?'

'I'm sick,' I said, keeping my eyes on Harley, but my peripheral vision totally checking out the guy behind.

He was tall and slim, this guy. He had dark, sandy-coloured hair, cut shortish, messy. He had a goatee (although it wasn't strictly a goatee; it was more of a barely noticeable not-shaved patch at his chin), blue eyes, a square jaw, and a ridiculously cute smile. He was wearing a pair of jeans that hung like washing clipped to his hip bones, and a checked shirt, with a jumper tied around his waist.

And he was chewing gum.

As it turns out, I'm a sucker for people chewing gum. Not all people. Most people look gross chewing gum. But when a cute guy walks into your house, with his jumper tied around his waist, and he kind of smiles, then he chews his gum, just one chew, in the back of his cheek, well, honestly, what's not to love?

'Oh, yeah, this is Seth,' Harley said, jabbing his thumb over his shoulder at the guy behind him. 'This is my sister, MC.'

'Hey,' Seth said.

He scratched his stomach, which was probably one of the sexiest things I'd ever seen: pushed up his shirt, just the tiniest bit, so that his stomach was right there on display like an advertisement. I felt myself staring as he ran his fingernails against his skin, then pushed his checked shirt down and got back to the matter at hand.

Which was standing in our kitchen, looking handsome.

Harley might have his faults as a brother, but he's always been pretty good at supplying me with Handsome Brother's Friends to eye off and crush on.

Jed who? I felt like saying to the world. *Jed the fuck who?*

'You don't look sick,' Harley said.

I shrugged. 'Didn't want to go to school.'

I could almost see the cogs in Harley's brain clicking over as he tried to figure out whether me staying home today had anything to do with me losing it with Nique on Saturday night, without being sure how to put it into words to actually ask me.

So instead he said, 'We're getting a burger. You wanna come?'

Could I be bothered? I'd have to have a shower, put on clean clothes, brush my teeth. But hello, Handsome Guy. 'Yeah,' I said. 'I'll go get dressed.'

We ate in, the three of us sitting around a cheap pine table in the fish-and-chip shop, chowing down on our burgers with the lot.

Seth dismantled his burger, pulling out the slice of beetroot and eating it on its own, then putting some chips in under the bun and starting to eat his new version, all the while scrolling through his feed.

'I can't believe people are still sending lolcats,' he said, looking at me, then at Harley. 'You know that chick Larissa from uni?' Harley nodded. 'Didn't lolcats die in the arse about five years ago? Seriously, Larissa,' he said, picking up his phone and speaking straight to the screen, as if he were on Facetime with her, 'you want to post lolcats, at least post one with attitude.'

Harley looked across at Seth. 'What you're saying is she needs more … cat-titude?' he asked, deadpan.

Harley had always been partial to the odd pun – it was something he got from Dad – but I couldn't believe he'd said something so lame in front of his cool-arse friend.

Seth ignored Harley's attempt at humour, as if he didn't want to embarrass him by acknowledging how truly bad it had been.

'No,' he said instead, shaking his head, 'what I'm saying is it has to be ... purrfect.' He grinned, then added, 'Sorry, just kitten around.'

Harley put his hand to his mouth like he was going to vomit. 'I'm fe-line sick from your terrible jokes.'

They both grinned at each other.

My brain started stumbling over everything kitten-like I could think of. Kitty litter. Mice. Fur.

'Personally, I thought it was clawsome,' Seth was saying to Harley.

'I'm all fur bad jokes,' Harley said back to him. 'But paw-lease.'

'You gotta admit, I'm pretty a-mew-sing,' Seth said.

It was like watching a tennis match – a rally that kept going, each lob sailing over the net; each time, one of them hitting it back. The two of them were grinning at each other like they were both champions.

And if I wasn't in love with Seth before we went to get a hamburger, I definitely was after that.

Chapter 15

I walked to the tram stop the next morning on my own.

I hadn't texted Liv back when she'd messaged me about catching the tram together. I still felt mad at her for being on Anouk's side. But I didn't care anymore about Anouk's party, about Jed. About any of it.

Because, as it turned out, a hamburger and a cute guy were all I'd needed to feel better.

Jed could have Whatshername, he could go for it. I had Seth.

Heart. Seth.

Well, I didn't *have* him, but I had spent an entire afternoon with him yesterday, and that had been a pretty good first step, I thought.

I felt a ping of irritation when I saw Liv sitting at the tram stop.

She looked up at me. 'I texted you,' she said.

'I didn't get your message,' I said.

She looked at me like she didn't believe me, but I didn't really care.

Be Anouk's best friend, I felt like saying to her. *I had a hamburger with a cute guy yesterday, and I'm not even going to tell you about it, because I don't tell stuff to people who defend Anouk. I only tell stuff to people who are my friends.*

We sat at the tram stop, both of us running our thumbs up our screens as we went through our feeds, me determined not to start a conversation. Then Liv looked across at me and said, 'Hey, I just remembered, you never finished telling me about the home invasion guy. You know, with your mum.'

I wanted to stay annoyed with her, wanted to hold a grudge against her – I hadn't forgiven her. But I started laughing, because I suddenly saw the whole thing all over again – me thinking through which moves I'd take him down with; the look on Mum's face when she saw me standing there – and the ridiculousness of it all suddenly hit me.

'Well, let's just say I was there in the bathroom, trying to work out which karate move I'm going to use on him for optimum damage, when he says to me, *Question: where's the toilet?* and apart from everything that was so cringey about the whole deal, who says "question" when they're about to ask a question? I mean, does he think I don't know the basics of conversation, so he has to explain what type of speech he's about to launch into, so I know what sort of answer I'm supposed to give?'

'Statement,' Liv said, holding up her finger at me. 'He sounds like a douche.'

'Complaint,' I added. 'He was buttoning up his shirt as he walked in on me as well.'

'Wondering out loud,' Liv said. 'Do you think he's from Tinder?'

'Temptation to vomit before answering,' I said. 'Gross. Yuck. Why would you even bring that up?'

And by the time we got to school, things almost felt back to normal.

Almost.

#

Anouk came up to me as we were all walking out to lunch.

'MC,' she said, putting her hand on my arm to stop me.

I stared at her, my eyes hardening into chips of flint.

'I just ...' She tipped her head back, as if the words she needed were written up there on the ceiling. Then she looked back at me. 'I just wanted to say ... I feel really bad that I didn't invite you to my party. You know, that I blocked you and everything.'

I chewed on my cheeks.

'It's just that ...' Again she searched the ceiling for clues then looked back at me, like this apology was killing her. 'I don't know. I think I felt like you didn't care less that I was into Jed. And making me go swimming on my own, it just felt really mean.'

'I didn't make you go swimming on your own,' I said, my fury rising red, like a thermometer going from zero to hero. 'I didn't want to go in, in the first place. You seem to keep forgetting that I said right from the start that I didn't want to do it. You make out like I deliberately stopped him from jumping in or something, but I didn't. He could have jumped or not jumped, it was up to him. Do you think I actually held on to him or something?'

She shook her head.

'No. I guess ... it's ... You know, anyway, it doesn't matter. Especially after I saw him with that other girl. I just thought: what are we even fighting about? That was why I sent you that photo. To say: what a douche; we're both idiots for liking him.'

I didn't answer her.

'Liv said yesterday,' she continued, filling the space between us with words, 'that you thought I was being sarcastic or something when I sent you that text from the party, but I wasn't.' I felt a chill down my spine at the thought of Liv telling Anouk what I'd said; filling Anouk in on how I felt. 'That was why I said "wish you were here" afterwards, because I really did. It wasn't the same without you.'

'Oh yeah, I'm sure you had a terrible time. I've seen the photos: you looked really sad.'

'I do. I wish you'd been there. It wasn't the same without you.'

I laughed. Or, more exhaled an irritated puff of air out my nose.

'Anouk, I don't even care,' I said and went out to the quad to sit down beside Yumi, clenching my jaw, crunching down on any words that might have wanted to escape; the parallels of my mouth holding firm against the thought that maybe, just maybe, she might be telling the truth.

Chapter 16

I've got a scholarship – I told you that already.

However, my scholarship-winning talents don't stretch to footy, which I played every Wednesday through winter.

I'd signed up because I'd thought it would be a bit of fun, but as it turned out, a lot of the girls who played were really serious about it, and really good at it. They kicked straight and true, goal after goal, and I spent at least two-quarters of every game on the interchange bench.

The Wednesday after Anouk's party, I was sitting on the bench, a blanket wrapped around my shoulders, watching everyone except me running around the oval while the coach discussed tactics with the assistant coach. They were pretending they hadn't noticed me – basically confirming that my sole purpose for the afternoon was to act as a spare body available to them in case someone came off injured.

There's nothing lonelier than the interchange bench during a game. Although at least spare body parts meant I served some purpose, which was more than I could have said about myself on the night of Anouk's party.

'MC,' I heard over my shoulder. I looked behind me.

Dad stood at the wire fence, his winter coat buttoned up and his collar tugged up around his ears.

'I had a spare afternoon,' he said. 'Thought I'd come and watch your game.'

Dad had never had a spare weekday afternoon, in all the time I'd known him. Which was all my life, duh.

'How did you know where I was playing?'

'Through my amazing powers of deduction. Also, I looked up your fixture.'

'Oh. Right.'

'I've texted you a few times this week,' he said to me.

I really didn't feel like rehashing Saturday night. And if he'd come to have another go at me, I wasn't interested.

I turned back to watch the game I wasn't required for.

'But it's okay,' he went on, speaking to my back. 'I called Mum, and she said you got home safely.'

His first time coming to watch a game of mine, and all he wanted to talk about was me not texting him back?

'You guys are doing well,' he said. I turned to see him pointing over my shoulder at the scoreboard, as if I didn't know where the score was written down.

'Ah, great goal,' he said, clapping his hands together, his gloves muffling the sound.

'Good hands,' he said a little later, when Liv went for the mark.

He provided a running commentary throughout the rest of the quarter, with me offering up the occasional 'yeah' and 'hm' and 'nice one' as I slowly got into the game, caught up by Dad's enthusiasm.

At the end of the second quarter, we all went into the changing room to hear the coach's 'rah rah, we're killing it, keep up the pressure, girls, yada yada', and then I got sent on ground for the last two quarters. (I think the fact that Dad was standing there made my coach feel like he had to be seen to be employing me in some capacity.)

After the game, Dad said he'd drive me home. I wanted to tell him he didn't need to; that I had two perfectly good legs that could get me where I wanted to go; that I'd catch the tram home with Liv.

That chivalry was dead.

But I was tired of being angry with him. With everyone. With the world. So I said yes.

We dropped in at a café on our way home, a whoomph of hot air hitting us as we walked through the door and into the electrically manufactured warmth. We sat down at a table and both of us studied the menu as if we were going to be tested on it later.

When I was a kid, I'd just unzip my brain to Dad, and whatever was in my head would tumble out for discussion. School, friends, tennis, running, drawing, telly, books, Harley, Mum, getting a dog, Disneyland, whales, dolphins, next holidays, whatever – it was all valid content.

But now that my skull was bulging like an overstuffed stocking, I couldn't think of a single thing to talk to him about.

A bowl of chips and a juice (me) and a beer (him) came to our table.

I pulled the longest, saltiest chip out and held it triumphantly up, pointing skyward, for him to envy, then chomped down on it. The hot soft centre of it burnt the roof of my mouth – divine retribution for my scalding words the other night.

'I'm sorry I got so angry the other night,' I mumbled.

Dad took a draught of his beer, then put the glass back down on the table, the two of us watching the bubbles fizzing.

'It's been hard for you these past few months,' he said, rubbing his finger down the glass and creating a path through the frost. 'It's taken a lot of adjusting. For all of us. You, me. Harley. Mum.'

He took a chip out of the bowl, not as big as mine, and put it in his mouth.

'And now' – he didn't look at me – 'the whole thing with Tosca, that adds a whole new dimension.'

I looked across at him.

Here we go, I thought to myself.

'What about Tosca?' I said, playing innocent. Pushing him to say the words. To tell me she was pregnant.

He looked up from his glass, straight at me.

'Well, as you noted the other night, she's my girlfriend.' He pursed his mouth. 'And the fact is …' Here he hesitated, grappling to fully put his mouth around what he had to say next. 'Well ... she's moved in with me. To the new house. I should have told you before now. I wanted to tell you. But it didn't seem the right time. But I should have told you.'

I didn't speak, waiting for him to tell me the rest of it. The pregnant bit. I selected another chip, the act of fishing out the fry giving me something to do.

'I know it probably seems rushed.' He sighed. 'You only met her a few weeks ago, and now here she is, moving in with me. But ... well, the fact is, we've been together for a while now. So while it might seem rushed, it's not really.'

I didn't say anything, still waiting for the next part. The Having a Baby part. But he didn't say anything else. That was it.

He reached into the bowl and grabbed the last big chip for himself, our hands brushing against each other as he took it out and held it level with my eyes.

'Mine,' he said.

'Hey! No fair.' I pouted.

'Ah, you're a chip off the old block,' he said to me, and put the chip in his mouth.

I looked at him and, despite his terrible dad joke, I laughed.

I'd seen the empty pack in the bin. But then I realised: a pregnancy test didn't necessarily equate to a pregnant person.

I felt the release in my shoulders as it settled into my brain that Tosca wasn't pregnant after all.

I wasn't much good at footy, but hell, I was scholarship-worthy at jumping to conclusions.

Chapter 17

A big group of us girls sat in the quad eating our lunch.

Everything was back to normal. Almost. It had been a couple of weeks since Anouk's party, and even though I still wasn't talking to her, things between us weren't as bitter as they had been. We were both starting to soften.

An announcement came over the intercom: 'Yumi Martin, please come to reception and pay for the pizza you ordered.'

Yumi looked up at the corner of the ceiling where the speaker was positioned, then looked around the table at us and shook her head. 'Good one, you guys.'

We all looked at her with our biggest, most innocent eyes.

'What?' Liv said. 'What are you talking about?'

'Apparently I ordered pizza?' Yumi said.

We all stayed silent.

'Fine,' she said, rising from the table and dragging Liv up by her shoulder, making her go to reception with her. 'I'll pay for it. But if any of you think you're having a slice,' she said over her shoulder as they walked up the stairs, 'you can think again. Because it's mine. All mine.'

We all burst into squeals of laughter, laughing even harder when they came back down the stairs with the gigantic, family-sized pizza box Liv and I had ordered in Yumi's name.

Yumi wouldn't let any of us have a slice for a couple of minutes, savouring each bite, making a big deal about how delicious it was, until in the end we all attacked the box and grabbed a piece for ourselves.

As we ate, Hattie told us what had happened to her the day before, her rushing voice slightly hampered by the pizza she was chewing on.

'... so I was sitting on the train, going into the city, and I saw this girl, and from the back she looked exactly like one of our neighbours – this chick called Mira, who used to live up the road from us.'

She barely took a breath before she went on, in true Hattie style.

'And I thought to myself, *That's Mira. I should say hi*, but I couldn't be bothered, because the train was about to arrive at the station, and I don't really know her that well, and we're not really friends, and I wasn't in the mood. So the train pulls in to Parliament, and this girl and I both get off, and I see that it isn't actually Mira.'

She looked at us to make sure we were keeping up, then ploughed on.

'So I thought, *Okay, right, well, she's not Mira, no drama*, catching the escalator up from the platform, la-di-da, and then this girl comes down the opposite escalator, going down to the platform I'd just come up from, and it was *actually* Mira.'

Hattie shook her head as if she still couldn't quite believe the craziness of the coincidence.

'And I stared at her, because it was so strange, and she saw me and waved and said hi, but we were on opposite escalators, so we couldn't talk or anything. But how weird is that? I'd been staring at the girl on the train, thinking about Mira, and then I get off the train and see Mira on the opposite escalator from me. I mean, what are the chances of that happening? It was completely bizarre. I kind of think maybe I should call her or something. But it's not like we were ever really good friends or anything. But ... so ... yeah, how big a coincidence is that? It was crazy. I feel like it must mean something, but I don't know what.'

I looked at Anouk, straight at her across the circle of our friends.

'Remember that weird thing with that photo you sent me last year?' I said to her.

Anouk looked at me but didn't answer. She wasn't going to join in. I realised that we were never going to be friends again; we'd gone too far along the not-friends road.

But then she nodded, and said, 'Yeah, that was weird,' and she grinned. 'MC was saying that she wanted to change her Facebook photo,' she went on, saying my name out loud for the first time in weeks, 'so I sent her through – as a joke – this photo of me from when I was a little kid, for her to use as her profile pic.'

I wanted to interrupt here, take up the thread of the story, but I decided that I'd leave it for her, the whole story, a gift from me to her.

'So MC is kind of laughing, and saying she'd use the photo, whatever' – and she looked at me and grinned again, a genuine, real grin, not a half-smile, not an avoiding of eyes – 'but then she looked at the photo, properly, and she saw …'

And here she left the space for me to fill in what had come next. A gift from her to me. A story we could tell together.

I took up the conversation thread.

'… in the background of the photo,' I said, 'standing behind Anouk, just as clear as you like, was my grandy, but this photo was from years earlier, when we didn't even know each other – me and Anouk, not me and Grandy, duh. And I said to Anouk, *Where was that photo taken?* because I thought, okay, it's probably not that strange, we all live in the same city, there's a fair chance Grandy would have been in the same park as Anouk at some stage, but then …'

And I handed back to Anouk.

'… well, yeah, the thing about that photo was that it wasn't taken here, at a park here, it was taken when we went to Canada to see some of Mum's family …'

'… and when I asked Grandpa about the time he and Grandy went to Canada, he said, *Oh, yes, that was a special treat. Grandy and I had never been overseas together before.* And so the thing is, what were the chances of Grandy being in the park at the same time as Anouk, in Canada …'

'... and it's not like we go to Canada every year or anything – we maybe go once every five years or something, to see Dad's family ...'

'... and for you to send me a photo, the one photo that has my grandy standing in it. And it's not like Grandy's standing staring at Anouk,' I explained to everyone. 'She's walking through the shot, looking at something completely different, but you can totally tell it's her ...'

'... and I mean, I don't even know what made me decide to send a photo of myself for MC's Facebook page ...'

'... and so yeah, I mean, that was pretty freaky.'

'I don't know what it means,' Anouk added, 'but yeah, it definitely means something.'

And we grinned at each other, and I thought to myself, *Maybe this is what it meant. This story. Here. Now. In front of everyone. Us. Going back to being friends.*

Maybe that was what that photo had been about.

A gift from Grandy to Anouk and me, all these years later.

♡ ◯ ↱

And then, three more weeks later

31ˢᵗ July

Better. Meet worse.

Chapter 18

It's possible to dress like a Melbourne train seat. And it only costs you thirty-eight dollars for the privilege.

Not that the fabric they use on Melbourne's train seats is particularly attractive. In fact, it's garish. 'Ugly' is another word that springs to mind. There's absolutely no reason you'd want to wear it.

Except for the fact that if you do, and then you go and sit on the train, it's all kinds of hilarious. Thirty-eight bucks' worth of serious belly laugh.

Yumi had stumbled across the T-shirt online a week or so earlier and ordered one, and on this particular mid-winter day in Melbourne, she'd decided that it needed an outing. On the train, of course. There was no point wearing it otherwise.

We walked down to the station – me, Liv and Yumi, all rugged up in our coats and jeans. We waited on the platform for the train into the city to arrive. Then we got on board, settled ourselves down, and Yumi took off her coat.

The three of us started laughing right away at the ridiculousness of it. Liv and I started taking shots – it was irresistible: Yumi staring deadpan at the camera, looking like she hadn't even noticed she was wearing a train seat cover as a T-shirt.

Liv and I posted shots on Insta and Snapchat, and behind us we could hear other people on the train laughing as they started taking photos of Yumi too. Yumi tilted her face at people's phones, wearing a wry smile, her T-shirt blending in perfectly with her surroundings.

#MelbourneTrainSeatFashionista

The likes started coming in pretty much immediately, the shares and comments, the distinctive notification *ding* of Insta lighting up my phone each time someone new reacted.

I posted the pics on Facebook as well, spreading the love. And it was as I was watching the likes and comments amass that I noticed something that chilled me far more than the nine-degree weather outside.

A friend of Harley's had shared something he'd seen on Buzzfeed – a still from a video of Emma Watson. The caption read: '17 Celebrities Who Hate All Things Anouk.'

I stared at Emma Watson. My chest felt crystalline, like my lungs had turned glassy and breakable.

Hate All Things Anouk.

I took a deep breath, trying to calm myself down.

Anouk was a super-common name in Norway. Every second person was probably called Anouk there. Emma Watson was probably making some movie in Norway, and this link had gone viral from there.

Nothing to do with me.

Besides, if my videos had been going to go viral (*as if*), it would have happened way back in June – not now, six weeks down the track.

I didn't click on the link. Not there in front of Liv and Yumi.

I'd check once I got home, but it wouldn't be anything to do with me. It was a coincidence. They weren't my videos.

Settle down, guilty conscience. Settle down.

My stomach churned for the entire rest of the trip into the city, but I couldn't get off the train and come home early, because our whole plan had been to catch the train into the city, then catch the train back out, Yumi in her glorious train-seat fashion for the entire trip. If I'd got off early, it would have seemed strange.

And all the way walking home from the train station, Liv and Yumi were with me, talking, laughing, checking out Insta and Snapchat, seeing how many people were liking the photos of Yumi in her train-seat T-shirt.

My glass lungs were having trouble drawing in air. A smile was frozen onto my face, and a fake laugh kept coming out of my mouth as Liv and Yumi showed me the comments that were coming up, and who'd shared what.

I needed to check Buzzfeed.

When we got to my place, I peeled off to go inside.

'What are you doing?' Yumi asked.

'Come to mine,' Liv said, dragging on my arm to bring me past my house and over to hers.

I shook my head. 'Can't,' I said. 'Mum said she needed me to do a couple of things at home. I have to go. I'll see you tomorrow.'

'But I haven't finished laughing yet,' Yumi said.

I shook my head. 'The laughs are officially over,' I said, wondering if that was truer than I'd meant it to be.

'I'm not catching the tram tomorrow,' Liv said. 'Mum's got a whole lot of stuff she has to take to the shop, so she said she'd drive me. You want a lift?'

I shook my head, barely even registering what she'd said. Now that I was so close to home, I couldn't focus on anything except clicking this Buzzfeed link. I needed to confirm it was a different Anouk before I'd be able to catch my breath properly.

I walked in the back door to see Seth sitting at the kitchen bench.

You see that? Seth was at our place. Again.

He seemed to have been around a lot over the past six weeks; often I'd get home from school of an afternoon and there he'd be, hanging in our lounge room, with that handsome face of his still as handsome as ever.

This particular afternoon, he was sitting at the kitchen bench, with maple syrup and cut-up lemons and icing sugar, and Harley next to him mixing up some pancake batter.

'Feel like a pancake?' Seth asked me.

So many reasons for a girl to hang and stay. So I hung and stayed.

I ate a maple-syruped pancake while I scrolled through my Facebook feed looking for the link I'd seen earlier that afternoon, only half-listening to Seth and Harley's banter.

And then I found her. Emma Watson.

'17 Celebrities who Hate All Things Anouk.'

I put my headphones in to drown out their voices, and clicked on the link. The page opened. And there they were – mine. All the rants I'd done about Anouk, the night of her party. Josh Hutcherson, the Queen of England, Jon Snow, Taylor Swift, ranting, 'Fook you Anouk, you fooking fook.' Justin Bieber calling her a sook. Kylie Jenner, Liam Hemsworth, Kendall Jenner.

All of them, all of me, swearing their heads off at Anouk.

It was worse than I could ever have imagined.

I left my pancake half eaten, and ran upstairs to my bedroom to delete agirlwalksintoaschool from Tumblr.

Chapter 19

There was a fair chance that some of my friends might have seen the Buzzfeed link – although maybe not, because it was a friend of Harley's who'd had it on his page, not a friend of mine.

But either way, without agirlwalksintoaschool on Tumblr, no one would be able to link it back to me.

All those things I'd written back in Year 9 – the moments when I'd been annoyed with Liv, pissed off with Yumi, angry at Anouk; the times when Hattie had given me the shits – had gone with the click of the delete button on my Tumblr dashboard yesterday. My rant about Anouk after Jed's party, from months back? Gone. All the stupid things I hadn't even remembered being annoyed about back in Year 9, those bytes of bitching? They'd been dragged out of the woods of millions of gig of data and thrown onto the scrap heap. Set fire to. All the evidence disposed of.

Regardless, I felt jittery that next morning. I'd barely been able to sleep, instead going over and over in my head all the different ways people might find the Buzzfeed article; what they'd say today at school; how Anouk would be about it; whether any of them would pick me as the one who'd started it.

I needed to be as normal as possible today.

Mum came into the kitchen in a pair of black pants, black heels and a white shirt, a colourful scarf tied at her neck.

If I was being normal, I'd have commented on the fact that she was all dressed up – much more dressed up than she normally was to work at Maude's shop.

I needed to practise being normal. Get in the swing of it. So I said, 'You look nice. Hot date?' and instantly regretted it, because the words 'hot' and 'date' then morphed inside my head to 'Tinder' and then to 'home invasion' and, yeah, even though it had been ages ago, I was still kind of scarred by it.

Mum smiled at me. 'Nope,' she said. 'I'm going back to school.'

I looked at her, then took my schoolbag off my shoulder and passed it over to her. 'Here you go,' I said. 'You're welcome.'

Normal.

She laughed. 'Sometimes the highlight of my day is making banana smoothies and crumpets for your afternoon tea,' she said. 'And Harley doesn't need me – not now that he's at uni. It's good working at the shop with Maude, but it's only a couple of days a week, and I've realised I need a bit more in my life.'

I smiled at her. 'Making smoothies is important work.'

She laughed. 'That's true. But I've become pretty good at making them over the years, and I think I'm ready for a new challenge.'

'That's great, Mum. Seriously. But if you change your mind,' I said, hitching my bag back onto my shoulder, about to head out the door, all the worry, all the dread still top of my mind despite me trying to sound normal, 'I don't mind staying home while you do my classes.'

'MC,' Mum said, stopping me. 'It's been tough the past few months, hasn't it?'

I looked at her.

'The past year, actually,' she corrected herself. 'It'll be a year in September, you know, since Dad moved out,' she added.

I knew exactly the day he'd moved out – September nineteenth, two weeks after my birthday.

I remembered thinking that good things always happened in threes. I'd turned sixteen on a Saturday. The following weekend, Mum, me, Liv and Prue had gone up the country to Daylesford for a girls-only couple of days. And then the following Saturday – the third Saturday in a row; *good things happen in threes* – Dad had called me and Harley into his study, because he had something he wanted to talk to us about. Mum had been in there too, waiting for us.

The way my luck had been going at the time, I'd honestly thought it wasn't out of the question that he was going to announce he'd booked us a trip to Disneyland. Of course, I was too old for Disney, but I gallantly decided that I was prepared to make an exception and go and have the most awesome time ever; do the old man a favour.

Shows how much I knew.

'Anyway,' Mum went on, rubbing down her white shirt and adjusting her scarf, 'I know I haven't been a great mum since he moved out. I kind of got myself into a bad mindset, thinking about Dad all the time, feeling angry that he had a new girlfriend – even feeling annoyed with you, every time you went over to see him, which I know isn't reasonable. I mean, he's your dad. Of course you want to see him.'

If I was honest, I had to admit I'd spent the past year blaming *her* for Dad leaving – thinking that if she'd been more like Tosca, younger, prettier, less naggy all the time, Dad wouldn't have moved out.

I thought about how much of the break-up I'd lain at her feet; the resentment I'd felt towards her about pretty much everything.

But it hadn't really been Mum's fault. It hadn't really been any of ours. Not even Dad's.

Dad had moved out because he'd met someone else and fallen in love with her. It was just bad luck that he'd met someone new when he already had a wife and kids.

The last ebb of anger drained out of me.

I thought about the videos I'd posted the night of Anouk's party. My Tumblr diary. Everything I'd spewed out online, and deleted last night. I felt like I'd been angry for months now and suddenly I realised that I didn't need to be. Everyone had shit times. It was just life.

My bag was still hoicked up onto my shoulder. I hadn't had a proper conversation with Mum in months. It hadn't always been like this; I'd used to adore her. I'd thought she was smart and pretty and funny. But then I'd got older, and everything had changed.

'It's great that you're going back to school,' I said. 'What are you going to study?'

'I'm going to business school,' she said. 'To retrain. I'll be learning some computer stuff – Powerpoint, Excel, that type of thing. It goes for a month, full-time, every day. And then I'm going to get myself a job.'

'Good on you. That's great.'

'And the other thing I wanted to tell you,' Mum went on, 'is that … I hope you don't mind, I know it might sound weird, or insensitive, and I don't mean it that way, but … I've decided I'm going to have a party, celebrating Dad leaving. Well, not exactly celebrating that he's gone – I still miss him; I feel jealous that he's found someone else, if I'm completely honest; that he's happy with someone else – but it's coming up to a year and I feel like I need to move on. So I'm going to have a party and celebrate the fact that I've got two beautiful kids, and I've got fantastic friends, and I have some great memories from my time spent with Dad. I thought maybe I'd have the party on the eighteenth of September, a year to the day, which is seven weeks away, and I wondered if you wanted to invite Liv and Yumi, and the three of you could serve drinks?'

Dad moving out had been one of the worst things to ever happen to me, and Mum wanted to celebrate? But I could see what she meant. She wanted to mark a line in the sand that signified we were moving on, still as a family, but a family in a different form. An 'X' marking the spot in the calendar where the new normal would properly start.

I looked at her. 'That's a good idea, Mum,' I finally said.

'Yeah,' she said, smiling back, looking relaxed and happy for the first time in ages. 'I think it is.'

#

Catching the tram in to school, me on my own without Liv, a shiver radiated all the way from my bones outwards to my skin. Maybe it was just the wintery Melbourne weather outside making me freezing – or maybe it was pure fear. It was hard to tell. All I knew was that my body was unable to stop shaking, and that the sense of frostiness was building as I got closer to school, a feeling of cold blueness pooling at my lips.

I had to keep reminding myself that there were literally millions and millions of bits of data on the internet. A little '17 Celebs' piece could easily be missed. There'd been nothing about it in any of my friends' feeds last night – just that one friend of Harley's yesterday afternoon. And I didn't even know him.

There was every chance they were going to miss it.

I got off the tram and buttoned up my school blazer, pulled my collar up, tried to ignore the seven-degree tentacles of cold as they did their best to crawl in under my clothes anyway. I walked in through the school gates.

Our school uniform is blue, with white pinstripes running through the fabric. If you tie your hair back in a ponytail or pigtails and you don't have an exact-same-shade-of-blue ribbon to tie it up with, you'll get a detention.

I looked down at my bare hands. My fingers were blue.

Walking down the corridor to my locker, I was hit in the eye with more blue, everywhere I looked – uniforms, ribbons, blue blue blue. It was blue overload.

Liv and Yumi and Anouk and Hattie and a few of the other girls were in the fully-blued-out corridor, staring into someone's phone, being knocked against as other girls walked past them.

Liv dragged me into the blue-on-blue group. 'You won't believe this,' she said, stepping back so I could get a good look at the screen. 'This is unbelievable.'

I took a deep breath.

I would believe it – because I knew exactly what I was about to see.

And, yep, there they were alright: seventeen celebrities, all hating on Anouk.

I felt my vision tunnel towards the phone, everything peripheral going hazy. The corridor felt crowded. Someone bumped past me and I felt a tectonic plate shift underneath me, leaving me and my friends on opposite sides of a gaping tear in the ground.

I fully expected them to turn towards me, a swooping of heads in my direction, as they said, *Did you do this? Was this you?*

I expected them to know, to guess, that it was because of me. Because of my Tumblr account.

My heart was banging – I could hardly get breath into my lungs. My teeth risked smashing because I was clenching my jaw so hard. My blue hands were gripping each other to stop the shaking.

I had to act surprised. Act like I'd never seen it before.

'Oh, wow, right,' I said, sliding a guilty look up at Anouk to see how she was reacting. But her eyes were completely absorbed by Taylor Swift and Kylie Jenner and Josh Hutcherson all saying, 'Fook you, Anouk, have a fooking sook.'

'What did you do to make them all so angry at you?' Liv said, her mouth splitting wide in a grin as she put her arm around Anouk. 'All these celebs. Whoa, I'm kind of impressed. It takes real star power to piss off that many people.'

'It's obviously not her,' I blurted, shaking my head at Liv.

'Well, duh,' Liv said. 'Thanks for that, Captain Obvious.'

'I thought you were special,' Yumi said to Anouk. 'That we were the only ones who said "fook Anouk". But now it turns out everyone says it. It's hilarious.'

'Well, it's a pretty obvious rhyme,' I said, talking loudly so they'd hear me over the noise of the corridor, jamming my frozen hands into my blazer pockets. 'I mean, as if we'd be the only ones to think of it.'

'But who's Anouk?' Hattie said, shaking her head. 'I've never heard of her. Is she, like, a singer, or an actor, or what?'

'Doesn't matter,' I said, feeling furious that they were spending so much time talking about it. 'She's obviously just some stupid Hollywood person we haven't heard about. Who cares.'

Hattie looked up, surprise glancing a blow across her face as she registered the edge in my voice.

'I mean, it's funny,' I added. *Normal. Remember normal.* 'But ... I think Emma Watson's doing a movie in Norway. I think I read that somewhere. I think that's where this has come from.'

'It's so strange,' Anouk said, shaking her head. 'So completely and utterly weird.'

I shrugged. 'I guess,' I said. And walked away from her, from all of them, towards class, gripping my folders so hard I could feel the indent the corners were making against my chest. It was the only way I could stop my hands from shaking.

I could hardly sit still in class. I had a distinct sense of ants crawling under my skin, nibbling bits off my spine to carry back to their nest. There was every chance my entire body was going to collapse from the press of my skin against the chewed-on bones.

Everyone spent morning break on their phones, scouring the internet for more Anouk stuff.

A couple of the celebrities in question had issued statements. Saying they hadn't been behind the videos; that they didn't even know an Anouk.

'Nothing from the Queen yet, though, I see,' said Liv drolly.

'She probably started it,' Yumi said. 'You know what she's like.'

'Come on, this is boring,' I said, wanting to take all their phones and smash them against the walls. 'Let's go do something.'

The problem was, we weren't the types of girls to go and play tennis or have a game of netball during lunch or recess. We were the hang-around-sitting-cross-legged-on-the-oval types. Sitting on our phones was exactly what we usually did.

#FookAnouk was trending all over the internet.

There were hundreds of fake celebrity rants. Taylor Lautner was pissed off that he'd been grounded by his parents for staying at a party past his curfew on the weekend. Demi Lovato was having a go at the person who'd stolen her carpark in the supermarket earlier that afternoon, and was all like, 'Seriously, that was so not okay. It was the complete opposite of okay. Whatever the opposite of okay is, that's what you did this afternoon, arsehole.' John Lennon was saying in a dodgy English accent that peace had no chance, what with the way things were going in the world at the moment. Ryan Gosling was hey girl-ing about the environment.

All of them hashtagged FookAnouk.

There were rhyming hashtags, too, which I might have found funny if it weren't for the teeth of the ants setting me on edge.

'My sister Britt likes to explain, in detail, every night over dinner, why @TheBachelor is superior television #ShitBritt #FookAnouk'

'My flatmate Andy has put up a shelf in our lounge room. It's crooked and things keep sliding off it, but still #HandyAndy #FookAnouk'

'My boyfriend Tucker just dumped me. While we were on holidays. In Paris #YouFuckerTucker #FookAnouk'

There was even a beer company that had posted a series of ads: different people happily holding their glasses aloft with the headline #FookAnouk and the tagline #CheersBeers.

To say that I didn't feel comfortable with any of it would be the understatement of the century.

The last class of the day was the longest of my life – fifty minutes of Mr Yumi going blah blah blah about *Jasper Jones*. I didn't care. Didn't care about Jasper Jones. Didn't care about the girl. Didn't care about any of it. I needed to get home so I could check that I was safe from the internet; that there was nothing anyone would find, no matter how many pages they trawled through. I needed to dig as deep online as I could.

When the bell rang, I didn't wait for Liv. I grabbed my bag from my locker and got to the tram stop in record time.

Even though I'd deleted everything on Tumblr, now this thing had got so big, I wondered fearfully what muddy digital footprints I might have left behind without meaning to.

When the tram arrived, I leapt aboard and took a seat near the front. I looked at the man sitting opposite me. He had the sort of eyebrows you wanted to take to with a pair of scissors, or a lawnmower.

I wanted to lean over and say to him, *Everyone gets annoyed with their friends, don't you reckon? It's totally normal to vent. Especially if you don't think they'll ever see it. I mean, imagine what my friends have written about me in their diaries over the years. It's just that my videos are doing the rounds of the internet, and their diaries aren't.*

I wanted to grab him by the shoulders, force him to look into my face. *Do I look like a bad person?* I wanted to say to him.

When I got home I went straight up to my room, flipped open my computer and keyed 'Fook Anouk' into Google.

There were 1,748,100 results.

There were links to the Buzzfeed story. Links to Reddit, YouTube. To 9GAG, Imgur, Facebook pages, an Irish radio station, Mediamass. IMDb. Some of them brought up the whole story reposted, with all seventeen celebrities ranting. Others had just cherry-picked individual rants and added their comments or content. Tonnes brought up brand-new material – hundreds of thousands of posts by hundreds of thousands of people I didn't know, with their own celebrities spouting their own messages to the world, all linking back to the original Buzzfeed story, to #FookAnouk – to my idea.

But when I keyed in specific details like 'Anouk,' 'MC' or 'agirlwalksintoaschool' nothing came up.

There was nothing that would lead to me. And nothing, therefore, that would lead to *my* Anouk.

Still, my body felt brittle with adrenaline and anxiety.

And I worried that it was all going to get so much worse.

#

I feigned another migraine the next day, didn't go to school. This time I actually did have a headache, though; I slept almost the whole day away.

That afternoon, Liv texted me to come over to her house. 'I know you're sick but Anouk's here,' she wrote. 'You gotta see this.'

'Anouk' and 'you gotta see this' weren't two statements I wanted to see together in the one sentence.

I couldn't not go, though. It would seem strange. Out of character. So I went over to Liv's and walked up to her bedroom. Anouk, Hattie, Liv and Yumi were all there – Anouk and Hattie on the bed, backs to the door, huddled over Anouk's phone; Yumi sitting atop Liv's desk, with Liv on her desk chair, both checking out Liv's laptop in her lap.

The four of them turned to look at me when I walked in, grins opening each of their faces. And then Anouk stood up and faced me, to show me the 'you gotta see this' factor I'd come over to see.

She was wearing a red-and-white striped T-shirt, the kind of thing Where's Wally would have worn, with big, bold, blocky type across the front saying: 'WHO THE FOOK IS ANOUK?' There was a Gig FM radio station logo underneath.

I felt my mouth falling open.

Someone was making T-shirts?

'What did you ... where ... I don't get it, did you find that online or something?' I said, trying to laugh, but finding myself unable to raise anything but a strangled choke.

'Gig is holding a competition,' Anouk said, holding out her phone so I could have a look at the website. 'They announced it this morning. You can win five thousand dollars if you find out who the real Anouk is.'

I couldn't find any words. It wasn't enough for everyone in the world to see my videos; to post their own videos, their own jokes? Everyone in the world wanted to know who the real Anouk was now, too?

I wanted to not be here. I wanted to be anywhere but here, in Liv's room, with poor Anouk wearing a 'Who the Fook is Anouk?' T-shirt and a five-thousand-dollar bounty on her unknowing head.

'I rang up just before,' Anouk went on, 'and told them I was an Anouk, so they said I could have a T-shirt for free, because I was the first Anouk who'd called in.'

My face felt radiator-hot. My stomach fell to my feet. My legs felt shaky. I said I needed to go to the toilet, then walked carefully, like I was drunk but trying to pretend I was sober, out of Liv's bedroom, straight past the bathroom, and home again without another word.

#

When I got home from Liv's I discovered that Gig FM weren't the only ones trying to find Anouk. There were radio stations from all over the world with a similar idea (but no T-shirt).

There was a morning show on American TV where the hosts had made it their own personal challenge to find out who Anouk was, and what she'd done to make the '17 celebrities' (all said with a wink at the camera) so angry at her.

Amsterdam seemed to have a glut of Anouks, all wearing a T-shirt that said 'Ik Ben Anouk'.

And the fake celebrities appearing all over the internet weren't ranting anymore – instead, they were yelling out,

'Annooouuukkk,' over and over, as if they were searching for her and hoping she'd answer.

Mum came to my doorway. 'MC,' she said. 'I've been calling you for ages. Dinner's ready.'

'I've got all this homework to do,' I said, feeling like millions more people were being packed into this snowball I'd created with every hit of the refresh button.

'Homework can wait,' Mum said, coming over and pushing my computer lid shut. 'You have to eat.'

'I'll eat in my room,' I said, opening my computer back up.

'No. If you're home, you eat with me.' Computer closed.

'Harley doesn't.' Computer open.

'Harley's not home.'

'Harley's never home, because why would he be?'

Mum sighed – heavily. I knew I was being bitchy, but I needed to stay with my computer; needed to watch things unfold. I needed to keep an eye on it, so I'd know when to take cover.

I could feel the breath of the internet – of the world – down the back of my neck.

Mum went downstairs, and I stayed on my computer. Pressed refresh. And there it was – on the first page.

A screen grab of agirlwalksintoaschool.

I reeled. There was no way it was still out there. I'd deleted it. But there it was – all the celeb vids, the accompanying hashtags I'd used – #PartyBitch, #MadAsHell, #TaylorSwift, #JustinBieber.

My video of the Gun was there too – #GirlsAreBitches.

All my stuff from Year 9 – my rants about Anouk (well, Annick back then) and Liv and Yumi and Hattie and all my other friends? Yep, that was there too. My entire blog screen-shotted, page by page, in all its hateful glory.

The first thing that had come up when I googled 'Fook Anouk'.

Chapter 20

I ran over to Liv's to try to sort things out – to explain that the videos had been a rant that I'd expected to go nowhere; that the rest of the blog, everything I'd written way back in Year 9, was all just stuff I'd written for no good reason other than that I'd been struggling with getting used to a new school.

'She's not home,' Prue said, frowning, then she put her hand on my arm. 'Are you okay, MC? You're shaking.'

'It's all fine,' I said, running backwards away from the door as I spoke, feeling an imperative to keep moving, to not be pinned down, to not have Prue's hand on my arm. 'Get Liv to call me as soon as she gets home,' I yelled.

Back at home, I banged the front door behind me like someone was chasing me. I rang Yumi, but her phone went straight to voicemail. Called Hattie.

Didn't have the guts to ring Anouk.

I kept picking my phone up, checking it, then putting it back down, then picking it back up again, to see if there were any texts, any alerts, what was happening on Snapchat and Insta and Facebook, if anyone had posted anything.

I checked each of my profiles to see if everyone was still my friend.

I went from my bedroom to the bathroom to my bedroom to the bathroom, in rotation. I wanted to get away from myself, but everywhere I looked, there I was.

A bit less than an hour later – who knew how many rotations I'd done between bedroom and bathroom by that stage, how many times I'd picked up my phone – Liv and Yumi and Hattie still hadn't called me, so I went back over to Liv's house. I couldn't stand being at home with myself. I needed to talk to her.

The light was on in her bedroom.

So I rang the doorbell.

Prue answered the door. Again.

'It's late,' she said to me, and I felt like there was an unfriendliness to her that I'd never seen before. Or a sadness maybe. 'Liv's gone to bed.'

'But it's only early. I need to speak to her.'

'It'll have to wait until tomorrow, I'm afraid. I don't know what's happened, but it's always better to talk things through when you're bright-eyed and bushy-tailed. You don't look bright-eyed at the moment. And Liv definitely doesn't look bushy-tailed.'

'But—'

'It has to wait, MC,' she repeated. 'Sort it out tomorrow at school.'

'Okay, well, tell Liv I'll come over tomorrow morning before school so we can catch the tram together.'

Prue looked away from the door, up the stairs towards Liv's room, then back at me. 'Okay,' she said. 'I'll let her know.' And then, as she was about to close the door, she said to me, 'It'll be fine, MC. Don't worry. I know it seems bad at the moment, but you girls will work it out.'

\#

When I went round to Liv's that next morning, she wasn't there. Prue's car was gone. Liv had been driven to school again.

Anything to avoid me.

As I sat on the tram, I watched the unfollows and unfriends, the deletes and blocks, start to cascade down my list of friends.

Instagram darkened with screenshots of agirlwalksinto aschool, shared again and again, by my friends, by strangers, the attached comments mounting: 'Your chance to win $5000' and 'I think I know these girls' and 'Five grand? Booyah!'

I worried that the tram might be involved in an horrific accident – that we'd all die, all the passengers, and I'd never get to school; would never get to fix any of this.

The world felt flimsy, like it was all balsa-wood facades and nothing behind. There was a staged quality to it.

I thought about what had happened with Yumi's mum the summer holidays before we started Year 10. One afternoon she was picking us all up from the beach and dropping us home, reminding us that we only had a few more days before school went back, teasing us that we were going to have to start getting used to getting up at seven o'clock again, saying how would we cope ... the next morning, she was riding with some of her cycling buddies at dawn and a car smashed into her and, bang, gone.

I remember that day with hyperclarity: where we'd been going, what we had planned, what I'd eaten for breakfast. I'd texted Yumi to see if she wanted to go to the beach again, and she hadn't answered. Liv had texted her. No answer. Then Prue came driving up to us, looking for us, chasing us down as we walked towards the tram stop, her face fallen, a greyness about her, and she told us to get in the car; said she needed to tell us something.

She took us back to my house, where Mum was in the kitchen, eyes red-rimmed. Then they told us that Yumi's mum had gone riding that morning. 'And, and ...' Liv's mum was shaking her head, as if she couldn't even get her mouth around the words, as if she didn't want to tell us the one thing she'd specifically brought us there for. 'And, I mean ...'

Liv and I both watching her, thinking, *What's her point? We want to get to the beach, we'll miss the tram, we're meeting people.*

'I'm afraid ...' Prue was still not able to get the words out. 'Well, the fact is ... this is very difficult to tell you, it's very distressing. Yumi's devastated, of course ...'

And then I started crying, even though I didn't know yet what she was talking about.

'... but you need to know ...'

Taking so long before she finally managed to tell us Yumi's mum had died.

I'd had the same feeling that day. That the world was untrustworthy. That it couldn't be relied upon to plod along, exactly as expected, rolling one day into another. That instead, you might wake up and Yumi's mum would be gone, just like that.

Or your dad might leave.

Or all your friends might hate you.

And there wasn't a thing you could do about it.

\#

I walked into a barricade of blue-jumpered backs at school. No one would even look at me.

'Anouk,' I said, trying to get to her, realising as I looked at her distressed face through the wall of my friends' backs the full extent of how badly I'd hurt her, how thoroughly I'd trashed our friendship, how awful it was that the entire globe was looking for her because of what I'd posted, that T-shirts were out in the world because of what I'd done.

That there was a five-thousand-dollar bounty on her head.

'I'm so sorry. I didn't ... it wasn't meant to ... I don't know how ...'

Hattie narrowed her eyes into slits at me, then put her arms around Anouk, shielding her from having me anywhere near her.

The bell rang, and everyone shoved past me, Anouk in the centre of the group like they were her security detail.

During maths, Yumi kept her hand up to her face so she didn't have to risk seeing even a fraction of me as we sat next to each other.

I couldn't even tell you whether it was statistics or logarithms that we were doing that day. I didn't hear any of it.

When the bell rang for morning recess, I gripped Yumi's arm as she stood up. 'Yumi,' I said. 'I know I fucked up. I know it's bad. But I ... please ...'

'Piss off, MC,' Liv said, coming over to the two of us.

'Liv, I just want to talk.'

'I'm pretty sure there's nothing you can say that I ever want to hear.'

'Please,' I said, grabbing Yumi again, knowing she was the most likely to soften. 'Please. I have to explain everything. Can we go to the oval?' I pleaded. 'Just for a second.'

Liv scoffed. 'You're hilarious.'

'I can't even imagine what you'd have to say,' Yumi said in a hurt whisper.

'Please?'

Yumi clasped her lips together tightly, like they were zipped, then finally unzipped them enough for a quiet, 'Okay,' to slip out.

The two of them grimly headed off towards the oval, with me following along a couple of steps behind, like they were the royal couple and I was the servant.

I could feel people watching us curiously as we walked through the quad. I could hear words like 'Tumblr' and 'agirlwalksintoaschool' and 'five grand' burbling up through the blueness.

'You've taken low to a whole new level,' Liv spat at me as soon as we'd sat down on the oval. 'All those videos, all those celebrities – I mean, one video would have been bad, but you seriously went to town. And now it's everywhere, and everyone wants to know who Anouk is, and what she did to make everyone so mad. There's all that shit you wrote on your stupid blog about how you should be able to kiss whoever you want, and calling her a Numero Uno Bitch – which she's totally not, but you definitely are. There's a pest control company which has a whole new campaign saying, "If you have any Anouks you want to get rid of, give us a call." There's this whole other thing on the internet now that's like, "My life might be turning to shit, but at least I don't have a friend like Anouk." And they don't even know her. It should be the other way around. *My life might be turning to shit, but at least I don't have a friend like MC.* That'd be more accurate.'

I pulled out clumps of the grass and looked at the bright green slivers clutched between my fingers.

'There's an entire site dedicated to guys saying, "Yes please, I'd like to Fook Anouk,"' Yumi added, 'with all this disgusting stuff about what they want to do if they get their hands on her. It's really scary.'

'It wasn't meant to go viral,' I protested. 'As if I wanted any of this happen.'

Yumi looked down at the lawn. 'Okay, so tell me, because I'm really dumb, what *did* you want to have happen when you posted all that stuff?'

The quietness, the sadness, the smudged freckle of her made me realise that there was no way of explaining any of this. Because it was all completely not okay.

'And then there's all that stuff you wrote about the rest of us,' Yumi added, her voice dropping to become even quieter. 'Making out like I don't have an opinion unless I check with Liv first.'

'As if Yumi checks anything with me,' Liv said furiously. 'What a fucked-up thing to say. It's like you've hated us all along, but we were all too stupid to realise.'

'How can you say I hate you?' I said weakly. 'You're my best friends.'

'And now all these people are texting Anouk,' Liv barrelled on, not listening to me, 'asking if she's the Anouk everyone's looking for, saying they want to cash in the five grand, and does she mind if everyone in the entire world knows who she is. She's literally ALL OVER THE INTERNET. So, yeah, fine then, I'm really interested to hear your explanation. Like, so curious you can't even begin to imagine.'

I thought back to Jed's party; to me jumping into the pool with him after Anouk had gone inside. Triggering this whole thing, like some intricate domino design that was impossible to predict until you stood back months later and saw how they'd all fallen.

I thought back to uploading those videos that night. The righteous fury I'd felt towards Anouk.

I hadn't intended for things to end up like this – for the internet to swarm all over her. That definitely wasn't the way I'd meant things to turn out.

But that wasn't an excuse, because everything I'd done, I'd done deliberately. I'd pushed over the first domino. I'd uploaded those videos. I hadn't known how it was going to pan out, but I'd started it.

'I ... wasn't invited to her party, and she sent that text of Jed and that girl, and I just felt really pissed off,' I muttered, the words sounding pathetic even to my own ears.

'Are you joking?' Liv said. 'Are you fucking kidding me?'

'I don't even remember writing half of it,' I said, pulling more grass out of the lawn. 'The stuff from Year 9, I mean. I didn't think anyone would ever see it. I'm so sorry.'

'So you go onto a little thing called the internet, because you don't want anyone to ever see it?' Liv said. 'Good plan.'

'I'm sure there have been things I've done that have pissed you guys off. You're just not stupid enough to get caught,' I protested.

'No,' Liv said, standing up and stepping away from me. 'No, actually, I'm so dumb, I always thought we were best friends. I never felt so annoyed with you, or so angry that I wanted to go onto the internet and vent to the world. But ... turns out I was wrong.'

'You're just ...' Yumi said, then she shook her head, as if there was no point in saying anything more, and stood up beside Liv.

The two of them walked away.

I sat alone on the oval and looked at the grip of grass I was holding in my hand. Like I was intent on destroying the school oval, one clumped handful at a time.

I didn't wait to see out the rest of that day's classes; didn't sign myself out. Didn't even go to my locker to get my things, just stood up from the oval, walked out the gate, caught the tram back home, and went up to my room.

Liv sent through a text at lunchtime. 'Sam Anderson from Year 12 just called Gig FM and scored herself $5000,' she wrote. 'Congratulations. You've officially ruined Anouk's life.'

So now all those creepy guys who'd written what they wanted to do to Anouk if they got their hands on her ... the pest control companies ... the breweries ... the celebs and the paparazzi ... the random commenters and sharers who all had an opinion even though it was none of their business and nothing to do with them ... they all knew who Anouk was.

And it was all my fault.

Mine and Sam Anderson's.

.

.

No.

Just mine.

I texted Anouk and said, 'I'm so sorry. I really didn't mean for any of this to happen. I'm so, so sorry. Sorry.'

I wanted to call her, talk to her in person, see how she was feeling, give her the opportunity to yell at me, but I knew that if I called, her phone would shunt me straight to voicemail.

I could picture her picking up her phone, seeing my name come up on her screen, and pressing the button to end my call.

Disconnecting me.

And fair enough, too. Because the entire world had turned itself southward-looking that afternoon after Gig FM announced it had found Anouk and she was a Melbourne girl.

Facebook hyperventilated from all the posts made by people I knew (on top of the millions made by people I didn't): comments like, 'Hang on. Our Anouk is the one the whole world's been looking for? Classic!' and, 'She's a couple of years above me at school,' and, 'I was at her party!' and reposts of my Tumblr blog with #MeanGirl, #FookAnouk, #PartyHag, #WhichOneOfAnouksFriendsWroteThisBlog.

Google Images had pages and pages and pages of shots from Anouk's party: pics of her in her wolf hat; shots of all of my (ex) friends in laughing groups; a sext she'd sent her old boyfriend in Year 10 of herself in her bra and undies.

#IdFookAnouk and #HesJustNotThatIntoAnouk were trending.

A new gossip column had sprung up titled 'Norway isn't as great as you think it is'. It had a photo of Anouk as its banner shot.

Nique had done a picture of a group of meerkats standing on their hind legs looking startled, with a banner across the top saying, 'When you're hangin' with da squad,' and underneath, 'and it turns out one of you is Anouk.'

It had been shared hundreds of thousands of times.

Anouk was now thoroughly entangled in the internet. Over ten million results came up when you googled her name. Complete strangers all had an opinion on her, and felt free to share it. Trolls were writing the most hideous, violent things about what they wanted to do to her.

And if the internet was chewing Anouk to bits, I couldn't even begin to imagine what was going to happen when it turned on me.

#

That night, Mum came up to my bedroom.

I was rolled up in a ball in bed, trying to keep as far away from my computer as possible. It was my new approach to dealing with the problem.

'I've just been on Facebook,' Mum said, sitting down on my bed.

I watched her from under my bedcovers. Didn't answer.

'Anouk's mum,' she went on, 'has done this post – which has been shared hundreds of times – saying that people all over the internet are talking about wanting to rape Anouk' – she stumbled, the words catching in her throat – 'and that it stems from something one of her friends did.'

Everything seemed dark in my room, shadowy, except this one spot I was focusing on – Mum's mouth. My room felt crowded with the two of us in there. Mum was taking up all the air. I could barely breathe. My chest felt sore. I wondered if sixteen was too young to have a heart attack.

'So then I went onto the internet,' Mum continued, although I could hardly hear her – it was like when you walk into a crowded party and all you can hear are clashing sounds and loud music, and no one person can be heard until your ears adjust to the new environment, 'and the things that are being written about Anouk are repulsive – violent, misogynistic, revolting – and there are all these celebrity videos where she's being abused, and apparently it all stems from a blog called agirlwalksintoaschool.'

My ears slowly adjusted.

'Which Prue tells me is yours,' she added.

I couldn't find the words to describe the hugeness of what I'd done. What a revolting person I was. The damage I'd caused, without even trying.

I put my hand over my face and shook my head back and forth.

'That it's something you did from when you first started at Whitbourn,' Mum went on, talking, talking, talking, but I didn't want to hear any more of it. My bedroom was supposed to be the one place I could escape to, but here she was, dragging all the horribleness in and dumping it on my doona, trying to talk at me through the webbing of my fingers, through the back-and-forth of my head.

I was feeling giddy from moving my head so much, which was good. I wanted to make myself sick.

Sick would be good.

'MC. Stop it.'

I kept my head moving, because I didn't want to hear another word.

Didn't want to hear. Didn't want to talk.

I'd been doing way too much talking lately – telling the world everything that came into my head. Every thought, every furious rant. Like everyone needed to hear my opinion on every little thing; on every person I knew. Well, I'd spoken my last words, they'd had maximum impact, and now I wasn't ever going to talk again. I was done with talking.

'I had no idea you had such a tough time when you first started there,' Mum said gently, putting her hand on mine to try to stop me moving my head. 'Why didn't you tell me?'

Tears were filling my head, like water in a bucket.

'Tell me what's been going on,' she pressed. 'We can sort this out. There are always two sides to a story.'

I took my hand away from my face and looked up at her, suddenly furious.

'Two sides?' I spat. 'No. My side's the same as everyone else's side. I'm a horrible person, I did a horrible thing, and it can't be fixed.'

'That's not true,' Mum said. 'You're not a horrible person. Don't say that. We can sort this out.'

'No,' I yelled. 'This can't be sorted out. It's unfixable. And I *am* a revolting person. You might as well get used to that fact.'

'Get dressed,' Mum said. 'We'll go over to Anouk's. We'll sit down, the four of us – you, me, Anouk and her mother – and we'll sort this out.'

I couldn't believe she was so dumb. 'What are you talking about?' I screamed at her. 'This is bigger than Anouk's house. Bigger than her street, bigger than the four of us sitting down together. This is worldwide. Don't you get it? What planet are you on? I've fucked up, and there's no way I can un-fuck it.'

And then I started crying.

And I couldn't stop.

#

In the end, Mum gave me a sleeping pill.

Apparently she'd been dosing herself up on these when Dad had first moved out. Which, from the way I was feeling, explained why she hadn't managed to get any cooking done and hadn't been bothered going outside to smoke her cigarettes.

My edges were fuzzy. I didn't really care about anything anymore. Or, no, that wasn't strictly true – I still cared, but I couldn't be bothered doing anything about it. Things could wash around me, life could troll along, could crush in on me, and so long as my edges were fuzzy, it just wouldn't matter, because I would give with every squeeze, like a marshmallow.

I vaguely heard Mum talking to Harley in the hallway outside my bedroom, telling him she was going over to Anouk's house to talk to her mum.

'Whoa,' I heard him say through my couldn't-care fog, 'what did you give her? She's off her face.'

I looked up at my ceiling and wished the flower mobile Dad had given me was still hanging there. This would have been the perfect time to look at it. But I'd taken it down, because … for some reason I couldn't even remember anymore.

Didn't matter.

Nothing mattered.

'You okay?' Harley said, coming in and standing over me, next to my bed.

'Great,' I said, my words barely audible, barely legible. 'Super-good. Super-better-good. Like, so great. So, so great.'

And then I turned to face the wall and felt tears roll out of the corners of my eyes and run into my hairline.

Chapter 21

I didn't wake up the next day until after eleven, even though I'd been in bed since the afternoon before; I'd kept drifting back to sleep, preferring it to real life.

When I finally did get up, I felt fuzzy from the sleeping pill Mum had given me. I didn't want to look at the internet, didn't want to see more damage but, like the night of Anouk's party, I felt compelled to delve in.

I pulled my laptop onto my knees.

And discovered that I was breaking news. Me and my school.

'Whitbourn Bullying Goes Viral' was the headline, with a photo of the front gates of our school boxed up next to it.

The story underneath basically bagged me from here to eternity.

'A series of offensive videos,' it said, 'simulating celebrities heaping a barrage of abuse upon a Whitbourn Grammar student has gone viral around the globe, with subsequent efforts set up worldwide to identify the student – including radio competitions in multiple countries, and a US talk-show segment – resulting in the naming of a Melbourne schoolgirl.'

I hated the way they used words like 'offensive' and 'barrage of abuse'. It was as if they were saying: *Here, this is what we think of this scumbag chick who uploaded the videos. Don't bother making up your own mind, because we've already made it up for you.*

I was pretty sure journalists weren't supposed to write like that – just the facts, wasn't that what they were supposed to report? Leave your opinions for the editorial page. Just the facts, please.

'A Melbourne mother spoke to this newspaper last night after her daughter was named as the infamous "Anouk" via the "Who the Fook is Anouk" Gig FM competition.

'"My daughter's real name isn't Anouk, by the way," clarified the mother, who requested neither she nor her daughter be named by this media outlet. Gig FM has also removed the victim's details from its website, due to the fact that she is a minor. "It's just a nickname the girls use for her. But for these vile videos to be out in the world, abusing my daughter, is contemptible. Absolutely revolting."

'The mother of the student who uploaded the videos – who this newspaper has also agreed not to name – apparently tried to defend the videos when she went to visit the victim's mother last night by saying they were "essentially harmless, but something that got a little out of control".

'"If that's considered harmless," the victim's mother said this morning, "I'd hate to see what bad behaviour looks like in that family. When a child can go on to the internet, basically destroy my daughter's reputation, and then her mother says it's harmless, well, words can't really describe how angry that makes me feel. I don't necessarily blame the school – I blame the parents. They've recently gone through a separation, so I feel sorry for them to a degree, but the fact remains: social media can be a vicious forum, and I'm determined something like this never happens again to any child. I expect the school to take this matter very seriously indeed. My daughter is completely devastated by what has happened to her. Not just the videos themselves but also the comments, the trolling she's being exposed to – this is vilification to the nth degree."

'One video showed Justin Bieber abusing "Anouk". Another video showed a painted portrait of Queen Elizabeth, a corgi on her lap, hurling abuse.

'The victim's mother said the videos were uploaded in response to a party her daughter held back in June.

'"If my daughter doesn't want to invite someone to her party, she's well within her rights. For these videos to be uploaded in response is bullying in the extreme."

'The mother of "Anouk" said her daughter came home from school yesterday at lunchtime distressed that she had been "outed" publicly on a radio station competition. The mother rang Whitbourn Grammar yesterday afternoon, but decided to go to the media after feeling frustrated when the principal refused to take immediate action.

'Headmistress Ruth Willis says she is taking the matter very seriously. At a hastily called school assembly this morning, she told all students that the videos are not a reflection of the type of values Whitbourn Grammar espouses.

'When contacted for comment this morning, Willis told this newspaper that respectful relationships were an important part of a Whitbourn education. "The girl who created the videos has been suspended for an indefinite period – I spoke to her parents and informed them of this earlier today – and the school is currently determining what ultimate punishment the student will receive."'

Suspended?

Nice to find out a little detail like that through the internet.

The comments at the bottom of the story ran for pages and pages – opinions voiced by people I didn't know, who didn't know me:

'Single-sex schools breed a particularly vicious type of child.'

And: 'If this were my child, I'd feel deeply ashamed.'

And: 'To think we're subsidising these schools. Disgraceful.'

Pure chemical anxiety coursed through my body, clogging up my chest and making me feel brittle as chalk. I read the article, the comments, again. And again. And again. A little sign to the side said '756 reading now'.

I'd unleashed a monster. I felt like an actual, physical creature was hunting me, stalking me, sniffing me out.

I'd made the biggest mistake of my life, and there was nothing I could do to fix it.

I was officially a Before and After type person.

Before Jed's party and After.

Before Anouk's party and After.

Before everything went viral.

And After.

#

We read a book earlier in the year for school – a great book – by this guy called Jim Crace. *Harvest*, it's called, and in it, an entire village turns on three travellers who have arrived looking for shelter, blames them for all the bad luck that has been happening, puts them into the stocks in the town square, and eventually kills them.

'Even though it's set in medieval days,' Mr Yumi had said to the class at the time, 'it's still just as relevant to society today. Through social media, people are jumping on bandwagons without knowing all the facts, making pronouncements, having loud opinions. People are losing their jobs because of it; some people have committed suicide. It's one of the most frightening aspects of social media: the public shaming. I want everyone to write a response to this book as if it were set in the current day – where instead of stocks and whipping posts, there's trolling and online harassment.'

In retrospect, I think he was trying to make the point that we need to think twice before putting things online.

Didn't sink in for me, clearly.

There had been an assumption, Mr Yumi told us, that village stocks and whipping posts stopped being a thing simply because cities got too big, town criers became obsolete, people got more sophisticated, the court system took over and people were judged according to a jury instead.

But, in fact, that wasn't why public shamings stopped.

Public shamings were outlawed because they were deemed too brutal. They extinguished self-respect. After being held in the stocks, or having their back whipped raw, or having their head shaved, instead of becoming good citizens, redeemed by the village punishment, the person who'd been shamed became lost to everyone and everything. Nothing mattered to them anymore. There was no going back, no redemption, no hope.

The things that had made life worth living for them were extinguished.

They became a person-shaped husk.

Press them too hard and they'd crumble to dust.

#

Mrs Willis came round to our house to officially tell me I'd been suspended. You know, just in case I hadn't already read all about it on the internet.

Harley and I sat on the couch watching the adults discuss my life, my doona wrapped around my shoulders and Harley's arm slung over the top, keeping my doona (and me) in place.

'As I said to you on the phone this morning,' Mum said to Mrs Willis as they sat in our lounge room, cups of tea on their laps, 'I understand why you're having to suspend MC, but the fact is, it didn't need to go this far – Frances didn't need to go to the media.'

Frances is Anouk's mum.

'I went over to talk to her last night about it all – I was very calm and reasonable – but she started yelling at me that I was as big a bully as my daughter, and that she was going public with it because of the school's refusal to punish MC harshly enough. And evidently it worked, because here you are.'

Neither of them spoke for a while.

'We've all been put in a very difficult position, now that the media's involved,' Mrs Willis said finally, shaking her head sadly. 'I'm hoping that today will be the worst of it. Tomorrow probably won't be great either, but hopefully by the beginning of next week something else will have taken over the front page.'

Poor, misguided Mrs Willis. As it turned out, she was dreaming.

After she left, Mum came and sat on the couch with Harley and me.

'I'm so sorry,' she said. 'I didn't fix things. I think I made it worse.'

I shook my head. 'You didn't make it worse. I'm the one who made it worse.'

She put her arms around me. 'You'll get through this,' she said. 'Things will be normal again in no time flat. You'll see.'

I sighed. Parents shouldn't make promises they can't keep.

#

Within hours of the newspaper story going to air, I'd been tied to every whipping post on the internet.

The fake celebrities now had a new focus: me. Angelina Jolie was surrounded by all these African kids, telling them, 'At least you don't have to go to school in Australia: they have people like MC over there.' Gollum was saying, 'MC.

Vi-cious,' hissing out the last part. Lana Del Rey was singing, 'I know you like the bad girls, honey, but seriously? You're with MC? That can't be true.'

My Facebook page wouldn't stay still long enough for me to actually be able to read all the posts pouring in from haters, trolls and people who used to be my friends.

'With friends like you, who needs enemies #PoorAnouk #MCwhataB'

'I still can't quite believe a friend of mine would do something like this #MCwhataB'

'You weren't invited to a party, so you do this? #Overreact Much? #MCwhataB'

'My flatmate wore my clothes (and wrecked them), stole my boyfriend, and set fire to our kitchen. But at least she's not #MCwhataB.'

'Some rando just drove into my car, then said it was my fault. But I guess I should be grateful. At least he's not #MCwhataB.'

Over and over. Thousands of comments.

MCwhataB.

MCwhataB.

MCwhataB.

There were also reams and reams of texts, emails and phone messages, almost all from numbers and accounts I didn't recognise – journalists and bloggers wanting to interview me, hear my side of the story; begging me to walk out of my front door so they could thrust microphones and cameras in my face, and get me to say something to fill their sites with.

Setting themselves up on our front lawn.

The first of them had driven up a little after lunch, parked his car and leant against his bonnet like a pigeon settling onto a powerline. Then another one had come. And another. And more and more of them, from the newspapers, the gossip mags, the daily talk shows – watching our house, talking to each other, lighting cigarettes, checking their phones, taking photos of our house, cawing and flapping while they waited for the chance of a juicy worm.

Me.

Apparently there was a matching set-up on Anouk's front lawn: journalists, camera and sound crews, all wanting to catch one or the other of us and plaster us all over the news.

I only knew about the matching set-up at Anouk's because of all the messages from people telling me that Anouk's front lawn was covered in people; that her life was now officially hell and it was all my fault. Even girls I'd never spoken to at school, people from my old school, friends of friends, felt free to send me messages and texts of abuse.

My phone, which had always felt like my lifeline, now felt like it was choking me.

I felt imprisoned. My room was suffocating me.

The front of my house felt like a flimsy barricade against all the people leaning against their cars wanting a piece of me.

I could hear Mum in her bedroom, talking on her phone. 'It's unbelievable,' she was saying. 'They've completely taken over the street … well, she's being very quiet, just lying in her room not saying much … Yes of course, it's very scary for her …'

I went downstairs to the kitchen, and opened the back door. Checked the garden. There were no sneaky journos trying to break in through the back.

I ran through our yard and hauled myself over the back fence, splinters from the wood palings catching in my hands. Then I ran down the driveway of the house behind us and onto the street.

I forced myself to walk. A running, crying teenager would have been too much of a beacon.

The street was empty of people anyway. *Hello*, it seemed to be saying, *just a normal school-day afternoon here. No one wants to interview anyone here, I'm afraid – not any of us here in our cheery homes, not creating havoc, not being hated by everyone in the entire world.*

I kept my eyes on my feet, to avoid making eye-contact with anyone even though there was no one here to make it with, my shoulders hunched inwards, trying to keep my body small. At the same time, I wanted to scream at all the houses for sitting there with their bricks-and-mortar coats, thinking they were so protective, that no one inside them would ever be hounded, ever feel pain – that none of their residents would ever feel enormous, un-turn-backable regret.

I turned down the next street, not even sure where I was headed. My entire body was on high alert, my eyes, ears, tongue, nose, skin, the entire length of me conscious of the streetscape, scanning, picking out any dangers and feeding them to my brain. This street seemed empty too, but I could feel eyes on me, watching me as I walked. I could feel my heart banging against my chest like it was trying to get out of there. My breathing was shallow, my body was sweating even though the day was so cold, and my mouth felt sucked dry of moisture.

My arms and legs were trembling.

I started running. As hard and as fast as I could.

I stumbled and fell. The heels of my palms were grazed and bloodied, gravel stuck there like it had been velcroed in. I was crying more tears than I'd even known were in my body, more tears than there were volumes of blood in my veins. I couldn't even imagine how one person could have so many tears in them, but they kept coming, more and more and more and more, like something out of *Alice in Wonderland* but without the trippy Cheshire Cat element.

Just me on the footpath with my scraped hands and no friends who would ever speak to me again.

I scrambled up and kept running, worried that someone was going to appear out of nowhere, jump on me, haul me up in front of the mob, lynch me, and put me in the stockade.

Running from the dangerous, buzzing swarm.

#

I ended up at the beach.

My palms stung from where I'd fallen over.

I sat on a stone wall and looked out over the water, occasionally bursting into tears and sobbing, then stopping, as if I was all cried out, then instantaneously exploding into sobs again a short time later.

I had no friends.

Everyone hated me.

Everyone.

My phone rang. Mum. I didn't answer it.

Mum again. I still didn't answer.

Dad called. I didn't answer.

Harley called. I answered.

'Where are you?' he said.

I realised I was crying so hard I was unable to get words out – the most basic task, the forming of a sentence, completely beyond me.

'I'll come and pick you up,' he said. 'Where are you?'

Crying, crying.

'Beach,' I managed.

'Near Head Street?' he asked.

I didn't know which one was Head Street. I didn't know where I was. My only signposts were water and sand and scrubby bushes. I could be anywhere. I felt completely disconnected from everything and everyone. I felt like I could disappear and that would be the best outcome – never to be seen again, never having to talk to anyone again, never anything.

'MC,' he said. 'I'm leaving now. I'll come find you. Just hold on. Sit tight. I'm coming now.'

#

You'd think sitting watching the water would have settled me.

It didn't. It made me feel worse. There was so much water, so much sand, so much sky, and me, alone.

I felt like I was crumpling in on myself. I kicked off my shoes. I could feel the winter dampness of the sand through my socks. I peeled them off. Took off my jumper. The frigid wind was harsh and exactly what I needed. Exactly right. Harsh was perfect.

I thought about Liv. Yumi. Anouk. Hattie. If I were them – if one of them had done a video like I had, had written things like I'd written on Tumblr – I would never want to speak to them again.

#MCwhataFriggingB.

My feet were freezing into feet-shaped blocks in the damp sand. I wanted the cold to reach inside me, so that all the heated feelings would become like nothing, frozen solid inside my chest.

I felt two hands clamp down on my shoulders and jumped away from whoever it was, frightened of what they might do to me – frightened that I was in danger from whoever it was who'd found me.

Whoever had recognised me.

'Hey,' Harley said, sitting down next to me. 'Shit. Sorry. Why have you got your shoes off? It's friggin' freezing!'

I didn't answer. I still felt like I didn't have any words left in me. Things were bad, they were worse than bad, and there was nothing I could do about it.

Everything was fucked.

Suddenly I realised that there was no point in caring. There was nothing I could do, and so nothing mattered. My phone rang again and I didn't even bother looking at it. It would be someone else I didn't know, wanting to ask me questions I didn't want to answer. Harley picked it up, then handed it to me.

'It's Yumi,' he said.

I looked at the screen and started crying again. Even the fact that she'd called was too much for me.

Harley answered it for me.

'Hey Yumi, it's Harley,' he said. Then he listened and I could hear a deep voice that didn't sound like Yumi saying something on the other end. 'Oh yeah, yeah, she's fine,' Harley said. 'I'm with her at the moment. We're down at the beach.' Silence. Listening. More silence. More listening. 'Yeah, thanks. Yeah, hold on, I'll put her on.'

And he handed the phone to me again, my sobs settling as I put the phone to my ear and said, 'Hey.'

'MC,' a man's voice said. 'It's Mr Yumi here. I asked Yumi if I could use her phone because I thought there was a chance you'd answer if you thought it was her. I've been trying to call you from the school phone all morning.'

I started crying again.

It wasn't Yumi.

Not Yumi at all.

'I wanted to check you're okay,' he went on. I nodded into the phone. 'We're all thinking of you. Mrs Willis said she was at your place earlier today. How are you going?'

I shook my head, starting to cry in earnest again.

'It can be a savage world sometimes,' he went on, and I could almost see him shaking his head as he said it, in that way he had when he was talking to us in class and someone had done or said something that monumentally disappointed him.

'Is Yumi there?' I managed to say. 'Can you put her on?'

There was a pause. And then he said, 'She's in class at the moment. Maybe I could bring her around to your place after school, so you can talk things through?'

I shook my head and handed the phone back to Harley. Yumi wouldn't come to see me. Mr Yumi had tricked me by calling on Yumi's phone. I'd always liked him, but now I realised he was like everyone else: not to be trusted, unsafe, calling me on Yumi's phone, making me think it was her when it wasn't.

'It's me again,' Harley said. 'Yeah, she's pretty upset ... I guess you could see how you go, but our front lawn is packed with journalists ... Yeah, maybe in a few days ...'

And I started crying all over again.

The sea air was so cold that it cut against my throat as I breathed it in. Once Harley had hung up, I turned my phone to silent, but left it face-up so we could see if any of the numbers were people we knew. People I might want to talk to. People like Yumi or Liv or Anouk.

It rang from an unfamiliar number.

Another unfamiliar number.

Another and another and another.

And then Grandpa called.

'Don't answer it,' I said.

'It's Grandpa. I can't not answer it.'

Harley picked it up. 'Hey, Grandpa,' he said.

I started crying again. Even the thought of Grandpa was too much for me at the moment.

'She's kind of busy right now – that's why I picked it up. How are things with you?'

He listened, then shook his head.

'No. She didn't go to school today. A couple of reasons.'

I could hear the deep burr of Grandpa's voice through the phone.

'Oh. Well, yeah, I guess. Is everything okay?' Harley asked, his voice going soft with concern.

I didn't think I could bear one more thing. I felt like my skeleton would shatter if even the tiniest, wafer-thin crumb of something else was put on my shoulders. I wasn't strong enough.

I was exhausted.

'Yeah, sure,' Harley said to Grandpa. 'We'll be round in a halfer.'

He hung up and looked at me.

'Grandpa has something he needs to talk to us about.'

#

I could drag it out, or I could tell it as it was.

Probably easier to tell it as it was.

We sat in Grandpa's kitchen as he made us a cup of tea and told us that Tosca had had a baby that day.

I didn't even know what to say.

It was impossible.

'He should have told you before now,' Grandpa said, putting cups of tea down in front of Harley and me and taking the lid off the sugar bowl. 'Dad should have. But they only found out quite late in the piece that she was pregnant, and then there were some complications with the baby.' He spooned sugar into his hot, milky tea. 'And in Dad's defence, she isn't supposed to be born for another three months – the baby isn't – so he probably thought he had plenty of time to break the news to you. But Tosca went into labour this morning and delivered a little girl. Milla.'

'No,' I said, shaking my head. 'That's impossible. I only saw Tosca recently. She didn't look anything like she was pregnant.'

Grandpa smiled sadly. 'Dad said he hasn't seen you much the last little while,' he said gently. 'When did you actually last see Tosca?'

I thought back. The last time I'd seen Tosca had been the night of Anouk's party. The night I'd seen the pregnancy kit in the bathroom rubbish bin.

'Okay . . . a while ago. But not that long ago,' I said limply.

If I was honest, I'd been avoiding Dad. He'd come to watch my footy a couple more times, taken time off work to see me, but I hadn't been round to their place again.

I'd been busy turning the entire world against me. That kind of thing took time and effort; it didn't just happen on its own.

'I saw her a couple of weeks ago,' Grandpa said, meaning Tosca, 'and she didn't look particularly pregnant to me either.

But as I said, the baby was born very prem. She hadn't started putting on her baby weight yet. The baby, I mean.'

A baby girl.

The fact that it was a girl made me feel punched in the guts. Why couldn't she have been a boy? I liked being Dad's girl; his only daughter. I knew it was ridiculous, but it mattered to me that she wasn't a boy. Because now this baby, this little girl, would be the one he'd throw onto his shoulders and walk down the street with, bending down so she didn't get smacked by trees. She'd be the one he'd plonk on his knee, whose back he'd draw on, whose swimming lessons he'd watch.

I didn't want him to have a new baby.

'There are problems, I'm afraid,' Grandpa went on, his eyes looking filmy. 'She's only a little tike, and she ... she might not make it, I'm afraid.'

Might not make it.

I watched Grandpa's face falling along his wrinkles, the weight of his sadness revealing in-depth each and every one of those lines. I put my hand up to cover my face. Tears streamed down my cheeks again. Just because I didn't want Dad to have a new baby didn't mean I wanted her to *die*. Why did everything I turn my mind to always turn to shit?

Poor Dad.

Poor Tosca.

Poor me.

Grandpa rubbed my back, comforting me. 'It'll be alright,' he kept repeating. 'You'll see, she'll be okay.'

My new baby sister might die, and my friends – and millions of online people – all hated me, and there were journalists camped out the front of our house and harassing Anouk, and it was all my fault, and I wasn't sure if I was able to cope anymore.

I heard Harley telling Grandpa that I'd been suspended; that there were journalists out the front of our house; that I was going through a pretty hard time; and I hunched my shoulders to make myself smaller so that the shame didn't have as large a target to splat all over.

'What do you mean, journalists out the front of your place? Why?' Grandpa asked, his hand stopping mid-rub as he tried to puzzle out what Harley was telling him.

'Long story,' Harley said.

'That's a disgrace. She's sixteen years old. They're animals. Don't give it another thought, darling. Stay here until whatever it is that's going on settles down,' Grandpa said. 'In your old room. Remember when you used to stay the night whenever Dad and Mum went out?' he said, getting back to rubbing up and down my spine.

I couldn't even smile at the memory. Basic social functions were becoming too much for me. I felt like everything from this morning, from the past few days, had an actual physical weight and was pressing down on me, preventing me from doing even the smallest of things.

'That's a brilliant idea,' Harley said. 'You should see how many of them are out the front. It's crazy.'

'Call Mum and get her to bring over your stuff,' Grandpa said.

'But then they'll follow her here,' I said, feeling like I was boxed in and whichever way I turned, the journalists were going to start swarming, ready to sting.

'Your mother's a smart woman,' Grandpa said. 'She'll figure it out.'

#

I was upstairs in my bedroom at Grandpa's, lying down on my old bed, when I heard a knock at the front door. I heard Harley go and open it; heard him talking quietly; heard Mum answering.

I heard her come up the stairs, then knock gently on my door, open it, step inside. I didn't want to see her. I felt overwhelmed with how much I'd messed up. With how much I'd let everyone down.

I looked at Mum and remembered that Tosca had a baby. I wondered how Mum would feel when she found out.

She sat down on my bed and put her hand on my feet. 'You okay?' she asked.

'They didn't follow you?'

'Are you joking? I'm a ninja mother. Good luck with catching me if I decide you're not going to.'

I sighed.

'How are you feeling?' she asked.

I nodded. Then I shook my head. Then I shrugged. Then I shook my head again.

She lay down on the bed beside me and stroked my hair. We hadn't lain like that for years. Not since I was a kid.

It felt weird.

But normal. A remembered type of normal.

She brushed my hair behind my ears.

'Why don't we do this anymore?' she said, looking up at the ceiling. 'Every morning, you used to come and sneak into bed with Dad and me. No matter whether we wanted you there or not, there you'd be, first thing, snuggling in between us. Remember that?'

It was like running down the corridor to see Dad every night when he'd come home from work – I hadn't realised it was something that would stop. It had seemed like it would last forever. And then, one day, I'd stopped wanting to go in there. I couldn't be bothered. I'd preferred lying in my own bed, reading my book, or looking up at the mobile hanging from my ceiling, thinking about stuff, just general, nothing stuff. I didn't wake up so early. By the time I opened my eyes, I could hear Mum rustling around in the kitchen, getting breakfast organised; Dad coming out of the shower, calling something down the stairs to Mum.

Now he had a new baby who was going to climb into bed with him in the mornings.

If she survived.

My friends were never going to speak to me again.

My life was worth nothing.

I could feel the heaviness sitting on my chest like a bale of hay, making it difficult for me to breathe.

I looked at the old tree out the window of my bedroom at Grandpa's. There were two knots on the trunk. If I tilted my head slightly, they looked like eyes – like the tree was looking down at me, watching over me. I'd looked at those eyes, watched the branches get broader, more spread out, over the years, and the eyes had always watched me. I wondered what the tree would have to say to me. But it didn't need to say anything. It needed to simply be where it was, its roots deep in the earth, and that was enough. It told me all about time, about seasons, things coming and things going.

'I should have told you about the baby,' Mum murmured. 'But Dad didn't want me to say anything, because Tosca had already had a few problems. He wanted to wait until she was a bit further down the track.'

'You knew?' I said.

'He told me a few weeks ago. I was upset at first, but then it helped me make a few decisions about my life. You know, going back to school, throwing the party. I realised, when he told me, that it really was over between us. And once I let go of it, I felt good. Better. You can't force someone to love you, or stay with you, or any of that. People stay together for all sorts of reasons, but they should never stay together if they're really not happy anymore. And he wasn't happy anymore. And actually, thinking about it now, I don't think I was either. I was bored.'

I closed my eyes, listening to the words forming in her chest before they came out of her mouth.

'Besides, I had good times with him. I probably had him in the best times, when he was young, when we did silly, crazy things. But sometimes a person falls out of love. And then maybe they fall in love with someone else. And even though I miss him, I'm happy that he's found someone else. I don't want bad things for him. I want him to be happy, and if Tosca makes him happy, then that's good.'

I kept my eyes closed, feeling tears dribbling down onto the pillow.

'Life keeps moving forward, whether you like it or not,' she said. 'I got an email today, about a job I've applied for. It's to be a Hansard reporter, in parliament. You know, taking down the notes of what everyone says, all the politicians, during question time. It'd be an amazing job, if I can get it. And I found out today that they want me to come in for an interview, which goes for three hours: there's a general knowledge test, and then I have to transcribe a speech, and then we have to analyse some news articles. A year ago, six months ago – three months ago, even – I would never have considered doing something like this. If Dad had stayed, I wouldn't have gone back and retrained. I wouldn't have applied for this job. I wouldn't have needed to. But it sounds really interesting, and I think it'll be great, if I can get it. So yeah, maybe Dad moving out isn't the worst thing that happened to me after all.'

I was feeling exhausted. I kept drifting in and out of what she was saying to me.

'Same with you,' she said to me, 'today. All this business with the videos and your friends and whatnot. All this will pass. Life has a way of turning out okay. Even if you think it's as bad as it can be, sometimes you look back on that time later and think to yourself, *Well, gee, that actually turned out to be a good thing.* You'll see. Everything will turn out okay ...'

And I didn't hear the rest of what she was saying, because I was asleep.

\#

When I woke up, Dad was sitting in my room, his laptop propped on his knee as he typed up some stuff. Work stuff, I guessed.

'Hey,' I said to him groggily.

He put his laptop down and came over to the bed to give me a kiss; put his hand on my forehead like he was checking my temperature.

'How are you feeling?' he said.

I shrugged.

I was feeling like shit, but I couldn't even be bothered going into that much detail. A shrug was as much effort as I could muster. I looked at him. He looked tired. Wrecked, actually. And then I remembered. He had a new baby. Dad and Tosca had a new baby. Milla.

'Congratulations,' I said. It sounded strange coming out of my mouth. 'How's ... Milla?'

That sounded even stranger. A brand-new name. My brand-new sister.

He leant his elbows heavily on his knees, clasping his hands in front of him like a prayer.

'She's having her first scan tomorrow,' he said. 'To see how she's doing.'

I felt bad that I hadn't spent more time with him these past weeks. If he hadn't come by to watch my footy those few times, I wouldn't have seen him at all.

'What sort of scan?' I asked.

'Brain scan,' he said.

'What for?'

He looked down at his hands. His prayerful hands.

'She's very prem,' he finally said, a ploddingness in each of his words. Like he felt the same as me – could barely be bothered to form the words inside his brain and push them out his mouth. 'The doctors have said she has something like a sixty per cent chance of surviving, and of that sixty per cent chance, there's something like a seventy-five per cent risk there'll be something seriously wrong with her. Permanently. If they don't give her enough oxygen, she could suffer brain damage. If she gets too much oxygen, she could go blind. It's a real balancing act for the doctors at the moment.'

He didn't say anything for a moment, collecting himself.

'So many terrible things for a tiny wee baby to have to deal with,' he said. 'I'm sorry you had to find out like this. That Tosca was pregnant.'

'It's okay,' I said, leaning over and putting my arms around him. I could hardly look at him when he seemed so fragile. It was like seeing him undressed, out of his suit, his emotions right there for anyone to see. 'I saw the pregnancy test, when I was over at your place all those weeks back.'

He puffed a slight laugh out his nose and sat back from me, his emotions back in their suit.

'You did, huh? Tosca said she'd left it in the bathroom rubbish bin. We hadn't expected you to come around, remember? And we'd only just found out. We were a bit shell-shocked ourselves.'

'But I don't understand. How can she have only found out two months ago, and now the baby's born? Milla's born?'

'Tosca was very sick when she was younger,' Dad said, the top button of his emotions undoing again. But just the top button this time. I could deal with that. 'She was in hospital for quite a long time. Missed out on a lot of school. The doctors told her she'd never be able to have a baby. She did keep saying to me that she thought she was putting on weight, but she didn't think anything of the periods she'd missed – they were never regular for her anyway, and she simply never considered the fact that she might be pregnant.'

'She wasn't looking fat when I saw her.'

Dad laughed, a full laugh this time. 'Well, she'll be pleased to hear that. She was, what, nearly twenty weeks when she finally did the test. The test you found. You wouldn't have expected her to look terribly pregnant at that stage.'

'Can I go see her?' I asked him.

'Milla?'

'Yeah. And Tosca.'

His face crumpled. And together, the two of us sat on my bed in my old bedroom at Grandpa's and mingled our tears, crying for each other, for ourselves, for Milla, for friendship, for all of it.

\#

Harley listened to all the messages on my phone for me and wrote down the details of every person. There were calls from TV journalists, the press, gossip mags and online sites, radio presenters, bloggers, vloggers. There were even messages from some celebrities – like Pip Quayle, and Esther Ruddick, and that cricketer who'd been slammed for being sexist.

Harley held my phone up to my ear and pressed replay on one of the messages.

'Hi, this is Brant Borgman with a message for MC.' I looked across at Harley, my heart perking up at hearing his cute English accent. 'I just wanted to say I know the media can be brutal. Though I can't even imagine how you're feeling at the moment. For what it's worth, I thought the videos were classic. If there's anything I can do to help, give me a call. My agent's number is …' And he recited a number. 'We're playing a gig in Melbourne tomorrow night,' he went on, 'if you want to come, and bring some friends. Backstage passes, of course.'

Backstage passes to see Brant Borgman and the Filthy Guys. Of course.

'You want me to call them back?' Harley asked. 'The Filthy Guys. Backstage passes.'

I shook my head. 'Nuh.'

'But you love the Filthy Guys,' he said.

'It's just a band,' I said. 'I don't really care.'

He looked at my phone, all the messages that still hadn't been answered, then put it down on the bed between us.

'I've got something to tell you,' he said, running his tongue over his lips, as if he were oiling them for the news he was about to tell me.

There was silence for a moment. Then a longer moment.

'I'm gay,' he said finally, 'and Seth is my … ahem, well, yeah … Seth is my boyfriend. I should have told you ages ago. But I'm just getting used to saying it myself. Hearing how it sounds coming out of my mouth. We've been together since uni started.'

Harley was gay?

But he didn't seem gay.

He didn't look gay.

And then I realised what a stupid thing that was to think. What did gay even look like?

'I wanted to tell you, but then I was worried about how it would change things,' Harley went on. 'And, you know, then Dad was off with Tosca, he was this big bad stud around town, and here I was, gay. And I feel so …' He sighed. 'I don't know. I mean, I don't think there's anything wrong with it, of course I don't, but, you know, we all grow up with fairytales about getting married and being dad, mum and the kids. Seth calls it my inner homophobe – he says I can't deal with the fact that I'm gay because I've got the fantasy in my head of how I'm supposed to be.'

'Your inner homophobe?'

He nodded.

'You're gay?'

He nodded again.

'But why haven't you told me till now?' I asked. 'As if I'd care.'

'Like I said, I'm kind of still getting used to it myself. Getting used to the idea that this isn't just a phase – it's real. I like guys. That's how I am.'

Harley bit his lip. I could see he was struggling with how much to say. How much to tell me.

'I got drunk on New Year's Eve,' Harley finally said quietly, 'and I made a move on Wilder.'

'Oh.'

'I was out of it,' he continued, 'and I thought I'd go for it. I'd liked him forever. What's not to love about Wilder, right? I wanted to be with him.'

He stopped talking, as if his breath had been taken away when he thought back to that night.

'And, I mean, he was kind of good about it,' he went on eventually. 'Said he didn't swing that way, didn't care if that's how I rolled, that it didn't change our friendship. But I felt like I'd been slapped. I was embarrassed. I'd misread him. I'd thought he liked me.'

'But Wilder does like you.'

'Not the way I liked him. And the next time I saw him, he was friendly, but you know, friendly. As in "friendly". There's nothing worse than "friendly" coming from a friend.'

I knew what he meant. When Liv had been all supportive after we'd first heard Anouk was having a party, I hadn't been able to stand it either.

Although, come to think of it, I could have done with supportive Liv right now.

'Things had changed,' Harley went on. 'Even though Wilder said it wasn't going to change things between us, it did. Of course it did. And I felt like he'd have told everyone, all the guys – all the people I'd been hanging out with since I was a kid, all of who would now be "friendly" towards me.'

He held his hands up in air quotes around 'friendly'. Harley has beautiful hands. Thin, elegant piano hands, my mum calls them.

I looked at my own hands, sitting in my lap. Turned them over like they were on a rotisserie. Examined them. Stared at them.

Hands are so weird. It's like they're completely independent from the rest of your body. You don't even have to think 'move now' or 'tap' or 'spread out like a sun' – they just do it, all on their own.

I noticed that my thumbnail was digging in under the nail of my middle finger on the other hand to scrape out a sliver of dirt.

'I went through a shitty time after that,' Harley said to me. 'Not as shitty as what you're going through at the moment, but definitely bad. I felt like no one was there for me.'

'That's not fair. I would have been there for you. It makes me sound like I'm a shitty sister. Then again, maybe I am. I'm a shitty friend. It makes sense that I'd be a shitty sister. Hashtag MC what a B.'

'You're not a shitty sister. You kept asking me, but I didn't want to tell. But then I started uni, and met some new people, met Seth, and yeah ... you know what? I'm happy.'

I tried to remember what happy felt like. It was hard to capture it.

'I remember,' Harley said, 'when everything happened with Wilder, it really got to me. They were my friends, my tribe, they'd kicked me out. I mean, not in so many words, but basically I felt completely alone.'

A calmness settled over me, Harley's arms around me, his energy reviving me.

'You know what happens when people reject you?' he asked me, his arms keeping me safe. 'Physically, what happens? We studied this in psych recently. It actually triggers the same part in the brain as a physical injury. And the reason it triggers that response is because back in the old days – you know, caveman days – if a caveman was kicked out of the tribe, he wouldn't survive. Not on his own. It was really important to stay in with the tribe. So the pain was a warning to change what you were doing, so you'd keep safe with the tribe.'

'But I can't change what I've done,' I said into his chest. 'I would – seriously, I promise, I would – but I can't. I can't do anything about it.'

'I know that,' he said, leaning back from me and checking my face, as if the pain and hurt would be appearing on my skin like bruises and lacerations. 'All I'm saying is, don't beat yourself up about it. It's going to hurt, literally, but maybe those friendships were getting to their use-by date anyway. You've been friends with those guys since forever. Maybe it's time to move on.'

I felt my face fall at the thought of not hanging out with them anymore.

'I couldn't imagine not being friends with Wilder and everyone,' he went on. 'But now I've got these fantastic new friends, and they know exactly who I am. They don't have a problem with the fact that I'm gay; that's just who I am. No biggie. You're a fantastic chick. You're smart, and you get along with everyone – you'll be fine.'

'Yeah, everyone. All my friends love me.'

'Usually,' he said, smiling down at me. 'Usually you get along with everyone. Don't do what I did and stay in your room the whole time thinking bad things about yourself. I can tell you for a fact: that's not the way to happiness. I considered dropping out of uni before I'd even started – that's how down I was. But something told me I should go anyway. And it was the best thing I could have done. Beating up on myself was not a good strategy. I don't want you doing that to yourself.'

'I can't imagine what it will be like when I go back to school,' I said.

'Don't worry about school. School is next week. Or the week after that. You want everything to go back to the way it's always been – but maybe the way it's always been wasn't as awesome as you thought it was. Maybe things can be better, and you just haven't seen the new better yet.'

I didn't want to hear any more. I knew he was trying to rally me, make me feel better, but I didn't.

I didn't feel better, and I couldn't fake it.

Chapter 22

Jed texted that afternoon. 'Whatcha doing?'

Yeah. Jed. After all these months.

I didn't answer.

He texted again. 'Are you ignoring me?'

After everything, here he was, on the end of a text, asking if I was ignoring him.

Like he hadn't ignored me since his party. Like he hadn't ruined my life.

But he was the only one nice enough to contact me now. And I was curious to know why. So I wrote, 'Where are you?'

'Down road from ur joint.'

'Where?'

'Park. With dog.'

'I'm not home. I'm at my grandpa's.'

'What park's near his place?'

I knew I shouldn't text him back. Didn't want to make things worse. But seriously, how much worse could they have got?

'McKeon Park,' I texted. 'U know it?'

'Sure. See you in 5.'

#

The Gun was running around the park when I got there, sniffing at the base of trees, looking up into the branches, checking for wildlife that might need taking down, fluffy possums that might be good to eat.

When Jed saw me, his eyes crinkled into a smile. Despite myself, I felt a skip in my chest. A bump. A jolt.

We walked around the park, me with my hands jammed into my pockets, him pushing the hair back behind my ear, putting his arms around my shoulders and bringing me in close to him, laughing, talking – acting normal. The weather was August-cold, bitter and icy, but without the pushy wind that had hassled everyone back in autumn.

It felt nice having Jed's body close to mine, keeping me warm. Hell, it felt nice to have anybody who wasn't a member of my direct family, and therefore forced to still love me, speaking to me at all.

We stopped at a bench under a big old tree. The branches of the tree cantilevered out over us, creating a leafy nook for us to nestle into.

When is a nook not a nook? When it's the name of a friend who I totally betrayed.

Jed dragged me to sit down next to him. Put his arm back around me, and took hold of my chin in his hands.

'Why haven't I seen you in so long?' he said.

I could feel my breath catching in my ribs.

'I saw those videos you posted,' he said. 'They were pretty funny.'

'Oh yeah,' I said, 'everyone thinks they're hilarious.'

'How about how viral it's gone? You couldn't have planned that, even if you'd tried.'

'Yeah, whoo hoo. Lucky me.'

'You're famous,' he said. And he leant forward and kissed me, pressing his lips against mine, messing with my head, wrecking my already-wrecked life. It felt so great. Just the two of us, his tongue and my tongue tasting each other, our bodies connecting first through our mouths, and then igniting along the points of contact between us. His arms, my shoulders. His hands running down my back. His thighs under my thighs as he pulled me to sit on his knee. His mouth pressing against my throat.

Like that night at his party.

The night that had started everything.

I pulled away and looked at him. 'You never called me,' I said.

'What are you talking about? I texted you just before,' he whispered, his mouth pushing back down onto my throat.

I felt that warmth, that *contact*, his mouth on my neck, and weakened again. Jed didn't hate me. Jed was speaking to me. More than speaking. He moved his mouth back up to mine and kissed me again, the two of us cushioned from the cold of the park, the warmth of our bodies heating up the air around us, creating our own external layer.

His hand moved under my jumper, under my shirt, finding the bare skin of my stomach, sliding behind to the bare skin of my back, and then creeping around again to my stomach, reaching up further under my jumper.

Someone in the distance whistled to their dog, the high pitch slipping into my ears and jagging my brain.

It occurred to me that I'd been hoping for him to say, *I called you plenty of times, but you never answered. You never called me back. All those messages I left you. I thought you weren't keen.*

Even after everything that had happened, I'd been hoping that. And I'd say to him, *My mum put a spy app on my phone, which meant I wasn't getting any of your messages.*

But no. He didn't say any of those things. Because he'd never called.

Harley was right. He wasn't that into me. It was only now, with everything that was going on, that he wanted to see me.

Because I was *famous.*

I pulled back from him. Pulled my jumper down. 'I have to go,' I said.

'Stay.' He pulled me back towards him.

I pulled myself back away. 'Seriously, I've got to go,' I repeated.

He folded his arms across his body to protect himself from the chill. The chill from me, or the chill from the weather, I wasn't sure which.

Jed had loomed huge in mine and Anouk's lives these past few months, and we hadn't even registered as a blip on his radar.

I shook my head. 'I can't believe you're what this is all about,' I said to him.

'What?'

'This whole thing, this fight with Anouk, all this stuff' – and I waved my arms around to show him that I was talking about everyone in the entire world who hated me, the suspension, the fallout from my friends – 'all for you.'

He grinned. 'I'm flattered,' he said, grabbing for my hand again.

'Omigod.' I yanked my hand out of his grip. 'It's not a compliment. I wouldn't be with you if you were the last guy on earth.'

He laughed. 'I'm pretty sure, if the whole of the human race depended on us for survival, you'd be with me.'

I walked out of the park.

Over him. Well and truly.

#

When I got back to Grandpa's, I opened up a whole new email.

'Dear Anouk,' I wrote, my thumbs jostling for position on the keyboard, 'I can't believe all of this was over Jed. If I had the choice now of swimming with you or Jed, I'd pick you every time. And not just because of how everything's turned out. I'd choose you because I know you'd be more fun to swim with – I'd have more laughs with you than I'd ever have with someone like him.

'You've always been one of my favourite people, and I can't believe I've hurt you so badly.

'The papers and your mum are right – I'm a bully. I just didn't realise it.

'Those videos were a horrible thing to send out into the world. And the stuff I wrote in my Year 9 diary – I mean, what sort of a person says that about her friends?

'I hacked your Facebook account the Monday after your party. Switched your language to Pirate English, liked all these bad products, poked all these guys.

'I'm a bully, and I hate that that's who I am.

'You probably won't believe that I didn't realise I was a bully. And fair enough. But honestly, I didn't think what I was doing was bullying. I just thought I was getting stuff off my chest.

'How piss-weak is that.

'It sounds like an excuse. The worst excuse ever.

'I don't expect you to reply to this.

'You might not even read it.

'But I needed to let you know that I've finally realised what sort of person I am.

'I'm so sorry.

'Love MC.'

Chapter 23

Mrs Willis had said she hoped something else would find its way onto the front page of the newspapers by Monday. And then I could come back to school.

Sorry, Mrs Willis, but welcome to my world of shit.

There were articles headlined 'Bullying is not just an "elite" problem' and 'Single-sex schools fail our girls' and 'Bullying with a $30,000 price tag'.

Apparently some parents had been ringing the school and threatening to withdraw their daughters; refusing to pay their school fees.

And then there was me. Sitting in Grandpa's front room, with Mrs Willis and Mum and Dad and Harley and Grandpa.

We couldn't meet up at school because of the press. Ditto our house – still. So Mum had suggested we meet at Grandpa's. I hated that Grandpa had to witness everything.

'I'm afraid,' Mrs Willis said, sitting on the couch, her hands fitting into each other like the clasp on a nanna bag, 'that … There's no easy way to say this. A decision's been made to ask MC to leave the school.'

I could feel my chest boom with the news.

It was as bad as it could be.

It couldn't be any worse.

'I'm really sorry,' Mrs Willis went on, 'but this business hasn't died down. Annick's mother isn't going to let it rest until some drastic action is taken.' She looked me in the eye. 'She wants you expelled, MC, and the board has decided that it's probably for the best.'

'Best for who?' Grandpa said.

'Best for the school,' Mrs Willis said. 'I'm not going to pretend this is the best for MC, because obviously the best thing would be for her to stay at school. I don't agree with the decision, but it's been taken out of my hands. The board has said they want her gone, and I only hold so much influence.'

You probably expect that I cried. I didn't. I didn't have any more tears left. No more sadness. I was empty.

'I don't want you to think we're abandoning her, though,' Mrs Willis went on. 'I'm speaking to—'

'This is your version of *not* abandoning her?' Mum said, interrupting Mrs Willis. 'Booting her out?'

Mrs Willis sighed. 'Julie,' she said, shrugging her shoulders, 'we're all trying our best. At the moment, I've managed to convince the board not to insist that you repay the school fees.

'What?' Dad said, his back straightening, as if he was ready for a fight.

'It would be very expensive if you had to pay back the fees,' Mrs Willis said. 'And I don't want that. But if you go public with any of these details, the board will expect you to repay.'

She shifted in her seat, like the couch had suddenly become uncomfortable.

'You can't be serious,' Mum said.

'What exactly are you trying to say?' Dad said at the same time.

'It's in the contract when you accept a scholarship,' Mrs Willis went on, 'that you "won't bring the school into disrepute", and if you do, that you'll repay the fees. It's all there, if you care to look it up. But the board has agreed to waive the fees. For the moment. So long as there's no further bad press.'

'You're bribing us,' Dad said.

'You're a lawyer,' Mrs Willis said, turning to him. 'What's the legal term for it? Whatever it is, let's settle for that.'

She put her hands up in two full halts, like a policewoman.

'I've spoken to a couple of the principals from other schools in the area,' she continued. 'Allumby and Belford Grammar have both indicated that they'd be happy to have a chat with MC and see if they can come to some sort of arrangement regarding next term. Of course, it won't be a scholarship, but it's as good an outcome as we can hope for. MC can complete her remaining Term 3 assignments from home, and submit them via Mr Martin.'

None of us said anything.

I wasn't going back to Whitbourn.

It was as big and as huge as that.

'I'll leave you to have a chat,' Mrs Willis said, standing up. 'I'm sorry it's such unhappy news, but hopefully one of those schools is of some interest to you. It will be in the papers tomorrow morning – the expulsion, I mean. And then, with luck, this whole episode will be put to bed. That's what I'm hoping, anyway.'

Dad and Grandpa walked Mrs Willis to the door.

'I can't believe this is the only solution,' Grandpa said. 'I know it's none of my business ...'

'Of course it's your business,' Mrs Willis said. 'She's your granddaughter.'

'... but expulsion seems so extreme.'

'Honestly,' Mrs Willis said, taking a deep breath, 'I think it's the only way we can throw cold water onto it. Once Annick's mother went public with this story and our school was splashed all over the headlines, we were hamstrung. Annick's mother has said she doesn't want Annick or her younger daughter having to spend one more day at school with MC there. She's not going to let up until MC has been expelled. We have no choice. It's the only way to get the media off our case. Give me a call tomorrow,' she said to Dad, turning away from Grandpa, 'and let me know if you want me to set up interviews with Allumby or Belford. Or both. And now, I'll leave you to it. Have a good evening.'

Chapter 24

Early the next morning, my phone rang. Yumi's name came up on my screen. I considered not picking it up. But of course I pressed 'accept'.

'It's me,' she said when I answered. Not in her usual Yumi voice – a bit quieter. Shyer, maybe.

'Hey,' I said.

'I'm at Liv's,' she said. 'We thought we might come over to yours.'

I laughed. 'Well, that'd be interesting. With all those journalists. Anyway, I'm not home. I'm at my grandpa's.'

'Oh. Okay. Well, do you feel like coming to my place instead?'

I wasn't sure if this was a joke. Was there a punchline I was bowling into? But I wanted to see them both. They were my best friends, and I missed them.

I hesitated. I wasn't sure I was ready for this.

But finally I said a small, 'Okay.'

And if there was a bigger punchline coming once I got round to Yumi's, I was just going to have to deal with it.

# #

Harley offered to drive me over there.

'I can walk, you know,' I said to him. 'It's not far.'

'No.' He shook his head. 'I want to see Wilder. All this, with you and your friends – it's made me realise how shit it is to not talk to a mate.'

I watched out the window of Harley's car as the traffic slid around us, people driving to wherever they were going, busy doing whatever they were doing, oblivious to the hell they'd heaped on me, the trolling, the comments, the opinions, even though here I was sitting in the lane next to them, a normal sixteen-year-old girl.

#MCwhataB.

'All this time,' Harley said, 'I'd assumed Wilder would have told everyone about what happened that night. But he didn't. Or, at least, I don't think he did. He didn't tell you, or Yumi. And when I think back, everyone else seemed confused about why I stopped seeing them; why I stopped replying to texts. I didn't handle it well. But I wasn't ready. And now, I'm ready. And, actually, everyone will be fine with it. I don't think anyone will judge me for it.'

'They definitely won't.'

'And if they do, fuck 'em.'

'Exactly.'

We went to the front door at Yumi's and knocked, neither of us feeling that we were back-door friends anymore.

Mr Yumi answered the door and stepped forward to give me a hug as soon as he saw me – a squeeze, like he was trying to wring the last of my tears out of me. Then he moved in and gave Harley a hug too.

'Been a while, mate,' he said.

'Yeah,' Harley said.

'Wilder's watching a movie out the back, if you want to go see him. The girls are up in Yumi's room,' he said to me.

But Wilder wasn't out the back. He was standing at the end of the hallway, grinning at Harley.

'What the fuck?' he said, coming down the hallway towards us. 'Since when do you use the front door?'

Harley smiled.

Wilder came up and put his arm around Harley's shoulder, dragging him away from me and down towards the back.

'You've missed me, I can tell,' I heard him saying to Harley. 'I can't say I'm surprised – you're only human.'

I watched them disappear into the belly of the house. I wasn't ready to move up into the second storey of Yumi's house yet.

'You okay?' Mr Yumi said to me.

I shrugged.

He put his arms around me again; then he released me and stepped back, so that I could walk up the stairs and into whatever came next.

I took the stairs one step at a time. Slowly. Reached the landing. Walked down the hallway and opened the door to Yumi's room.

Liv was there. Yumi was.

And so were Anouk and Hattie.

Hello, punchline.

My eyes filled up with tears. I'd never cried so much in my entire life. I felt like this would never end. But instead of letting the tears fall, I pushed them away with the heel of my hand, and looked at the four of them.

'You've been expelled,' Liv said, leaning against Yumi's desk and looking at the floor.

'Yeah ...' And I wanted to add that Anouk's mum must be feeling pretty happy, now that she'd got rid of me. Now that Anouk and her sister didn't have to run into me in the schoolyard anymore. But then I realised that was my problem. I'd always felt like I could vent whenever I wanted to. But maybe that wasn't right. Maybe I didn't have to tell everyone every single thing that was rotating inside my head – just the important stuff. Maybe I could take that sarcastic comment or the bitchy remark that was clanging against my brain, and instead of venting on the internet, I could put it in a box and lock the box, then take the box out of my head and put it in a cupboard, and shut the cupboard and not open it again until the bitchy comment had shrivelled up into nothing.

'Yeah,' I said simply. 'Me and Whitbourn, no more.'

Anouk started crying. 'I got your email,' she said.

And then, like a Mexican wave rippling through the room, the rest of us were all crying too – me, Yumi, Liv, Hattie, all five of us. I went over and put my arms around Anouk, the two of us sobbing into each other's shoulders.

'I'm so sorry,' I said to her. 'I can't believe I did this to you.'

'No,' she said, shaking her head against my ear. 'I can't believe she's done this – my mum. Everyone's saying to her, *You're a warrior mama*, and I know she was only trying to protect me, but because she went to the media she's actually ruined your life. I can't believe you've been expelled.'

'But she's right,' I sobbed, feeling the weight of everything draining out of me as I kept my arms around Anouk. 'I'm a bully. I just honestly didn't realise that I was. When I did those videos that night ...'

'I can't believe I didn't invite you.'

'... I kind of, I don't know, it's all stuff I would never have said to your face. But for some reason, I felt like I could put it out on the internet and that would be fine. And now you've got all the press out the front of your house, all that stuff happening online. I mean, shit, I can't believe I've put you through that. And all because of stupid Jed.'

Anouk shook her head; I felt the movement of it against my collarbone.

'He called me, you know,' she finally said, stepping back from me. 'After I was outed as the Anouk everyone was looking for.'

Of course he would have called her. Of *course* he would have called.

'We went and got a coffee,' she continued. 'He said all this stuff, about how cool it was that I was all over the internet; about how he'd always liked me. He started talking about Merimbula, you know – *remember this, remember that* – and as we sat there I realised that the only reason he'd called me was because I was the girl from the internet. Because I was "trending".'

I didn't answer for a moment. And then I said, 'He called me too.'

Anouk grinned at me. 'Because you'd become a hashtag?'

I nodded.

'Seriously, what a douchebag,' Yumi said. Her first words since I'd entered the room.

'He's such a dick,' Hattie agreed.

I felt tears well up in my eyes again.

'But now the trolls, the press, all the stuff I've put you through,' I said to Anouk, my chin crumpling. 'I'm so sorry. I don't blame you for hating me.'

'I don't hate you,' Anouk said. 'It was bad at first, I'll admit. All those creepy guys online saying all the gross stuff they wanted to do to me, it freaked me out. But Mrs Willis organised for the tech guy from school to delete all my accounts – I didn't even see half the stuff that was written about me in the end – and I've got a whole new bunch of accounts set up, so it doesn't really matter. For all the new accounts, I'm back to being Annick. And Jed? Not on my list of contacts.'

She took a step back and looked at me.

'But you: definitely back on there. You weren't the only one who did the wrong thing. I was a bitch too. As for the press, well, there are only a couple of them left,' she said. She was still holding my hands. 'Mum went psycho at them this morning. She told them it was all over, that you weren't coming back to the school, so that was that. Also, I think there's been a pretty big backlash against them, against the media, because we're still schoolkids. Everyone's being all like, *Hey, lay off the kids.* And the funny thing is, after Mum went off, they just kind of packed up their gear and left. You know what Mum's like. You wouldn't get in an argument with her.'

'I'll say,' I said, laughing and crying at the same time.

'Oh God,' Anouk said, her hands going up to cover her mouth. 'I shouldn't have said that.'

'No!' I was more laughing than crying now. 'I'm joking. There aren't as many at our place either apparently, Mum said. I think maybe it's all kind of winding up. They know who we are. They know what I did. Know I'm a massive bitch. End of story.'

'You're not a massive bitch,' Anouk said.

'Are you joking?' Liv said, looking into my eyes and grinning. 'She's a totally massive bitch. She's even got a hashtag to prove it.'

It was so good to have Sarcastic Liv back on board.

♡ ⚬ ↗

Six weeks later

19th September

Claudie and me

Chapter 25

My version of a party is this: a bunch of people chucked in together, music cranked up, cute boys (with fifty bonus points if you kiss one of them), dance-face with Liv, selfies, photos, noise, mayhem, no parents.

Mum's version is pretty different. First up: there's food. Lots of it. Clearly, when you're older you like eating a bunch of stuff – she'd made a lasagne, chicken sandwiches, sausage rolls, party pies, baguettes sliced then slathered with pickles and ham. Plus sushi and sashimi, brought by Maude, and tiers of cupcakes, baked, iced and decorated by Prue herself.

Liv, Yumi, Anouk, Hattie and I were given instructions on what to heat up when, how to slice things up (like that was hard), and in what order to bring things out to the party. Sushi and sashimi were first; chicken sambos next; lasagne, party pies and sausage rolls after that. The cupcakes were to be brought out and put on the table around ten; then, weirdly, the pickles-and-ham baguettes were for later in the night, 'when everyone's getting peckish again'.

I felt confident no one would be feeling peckish later in the night if they went through all that food beforehand, but as I said, parents party differently.

Anouk's mum hadn't wanted Anouk to come, of course. But Anouk had said it was bad luck, she was coming anyway.

I think Mum felt a bit weird when Anouk arrived, but she simply gave her a hug and said, 'Nice to see you,' even though I'm not sure she really meant it.

Harley and Seth and Wilder were serving behind the bar, under strict instructions to not drink its entire contents.

Mum had originally said she'd cancel her party, what with me being expelled and all six weeks ago, but I'd told her I wanted her to go ahead with it. It seemed important that she have it on the anniversary of the day Dad had moved out, and really I was just as keen to have something to celebrate as she was.

Mum was wearing a navy-blue dress with black stockings and black shoes and her hair pulled up off her face in a casual bun at the back.

'You scrubbed up alright for an old bird,' Maude said.

Maude was wearing an animal-print kaftan with bling sewn around the neckline and flat sandals. Prue was wearing a black-and-white dress, with her hair blow-dried and big dangly earrings – which looked like they were mine ... Actually, they were definitely mine, but I didn't want to say anything because she'd probably got them from Liv's room, and Liv would have got them from me at some stage, and none of it mattered anyway.

There were other friends of Mum's – her old schoolfriends; Tim, who Mum used to work with; and a bunch of other people I didn't know, but who all seemed to know exactly who I was, and told me how pretty I was, how much like Mum I was, some of them asking how Dad was going, like it was all very friendly.

Things are still nuclear, I felt like telling them. And then I realised, as I looked around the room, that actually, things weren't nuclear anymore. Things were fine.

A mushroom cloud lifted from my shoulders and drifted out the front door, which had been left propped open so that Mum didn't have to keep going and opening it every time a new person rocked up.

She got that Hansard job, by the way – Mum did. She loves it. Parliament only sits every second week, but when it's on, she's there no matter till what time. Sometimes she doesn't finish until three o'clock in the morning, and then she's straight back in there at nine the next day.

But she's happy. Things are good for her.

Milla is six weeks old now, and still tiny and frail. Harley and I have been to see her in the hospital, washing our hands for a full two minutes each time before we're allowed into NICU.

The Neonatal Intensive Care Unit.

The things I know now that I didn't know six weeks ago.

She's in a humidicrib. We aren't allowed to touch her or hold her. Her skin is kind of sticky-looking, but that's because she's so prem. There are still no guarantees, but we're hoping she's going to be okay. She seems good so far.

I went for interviews at Allumby and Belford, too.

They both seemed good, but there was something about Allumby that I preferred.

Nicer uniforms, for one.

And something else, as well. During our interview, the headmistress there, Mrs Ralston, made a comment that stuck with me.

She said, 'All these people pay lip-service to the fact that the human brain isn't fully developed until you're in your mid-twenties, but as soon as a teenager steps out of line, does something regrettable, everyone comes down on them like a ton of bricks.'

It wasn't that she was saying what I'd done was okay, and she wasn't making excuses for me, but 'regrettable' sounded a whole lot more gentle than some of the stuff I'd seen written about me.

So, I start at Allumby on the first day of Term 4.

'Allumby on a Mond'y,' as Liv keeps saying.

I worry about how it will be. I imagine turning up there in my new uniform; sitting at a desk next to someone I don't know, in a class full of girls I don't know. I wonder if they'll figure out I was the one who started the whole fook Anouk thing. They'll at least think it's strange that I'm changing schools this late in the year. But they might assume it's for some other, boring reason – that we've come from interstate or something – and just not ask. I remember that happened last year at Whitbourn: Emily Maton came to school, stood up the front of English, was introduced by the teacher, and that was it. New girl officially a part of our year level. I still don't know why she moved schools.

Oh. And I've changed all my social media accounts, of course.

Changed my name, too.

That's the kind of thing a person does when they become a hashtag.

It feels weird not thinking of myself as MC anymore, but I'm getting used to it. I considered going with Marie-Claude (seeing as it's on my birth certificate), but it's such a mouthful and I've never really liked it. Then I thought maybe I'd go with the first part, the Marie bit, but it didn't sit well inside my head or in my mouth.

Hi, I'm Marie.

No.

So instead, I've gone with Claudie.

I like it.

Claudie sounds like the sort of person I might want to be friends with. Claudie sounds like she's been through a few things, but they've made her a better, stronger person.

So yeah, hi. Pleased to meet you. I'm Claudie. I start at Allumby in three Mond'ies' time.

I've got a good feeling about how it's all going to pan out.

Acknowledgements

This book started off as one idea, then morphed into something else entirely. But the person who was there at the beginning and who made me think the little nugget of an idea was worth pursuing was Kirsty Eagar. For your enthusiasm and continual, genuine encouragement, Kirsty, I thank you.

Thanks also to Kim Kane for being a good enough friend to counsel me on whether a sequel to *The Guy, the Girl* was begging to be written. It wasn't. I owe you.

To my incredible publisher, Anna McFarlane, and my brilliant editor, Elise Jones, enormous, gigantic thanks. Both your names should be on the front cover, because you took my idea and pushed it in directions that surprised and delighted (and exhausted) me. I'd trust both of you with a red pen (or a glass of red wine) anytime. Thanks also to the rest of the amazing team at Allen & Unwin – the clever folk in the sales, marketing and art departments, especially Debra Billson for a cover design that I completely and utterly love.

As always, I want to thank all my friends and family who have supported me through each of my books, especially my gorgeous husband, Andrew, who believes in me a hundred per cent, and my three beautiful children, who show me where the stories are, without even realising they're doing it.

Thanks to my early readers, who endured various stages of awfulness: Susan Stevenson, Andrew Williams, Natalie Platten, Della Sholl, Audrey McCullough, Sally Fetherstonhaugh, Kate McCullough, Marylou O'Brien, Andrew Borg and Savannah Indigo. Also, thanks to Andrew Borg, Savannah Indigo, Chiara Yiontis and Charlie Williams for detailing the nuanced politics of social media to me, and to James Blake for letting me steal his #TrainSeatFashion idea for my own writing purposes.

Thanks to Varuna the Writers' House for an amazing fortnight. Two weeks' worth of concentrated writing, cooked meals and fireside chats with Anita Smith and Natalie Kestecher helped me get this book into a shape I was happy with.

Thanks to Jon Ronson for his most excellent *So You've Been Publicly Shamed*, which inspired this book. Thanks to *This American Life* for a podcast filled with coincidences, which kickstarted my story of Anouk and MC's reconciliation.

Thanks to all the staff at Readings bookshops – especially Bernard Vella, Athina Clarke, Susan Stevenson, Alice Bisits, Daniella Robertson, Andrew Borg, Jackie Redlich and Alistair Mathieson-Lynn – for their unwavering support of me and my writing. You don't get to be Official Best Bookshop in the World without great people, and Readings is full of them.

Love and thanks to all my #LoveOzYA friends – with a special shout-out to Fiona Wood. Your friendships are an unexpected bonus of writing for young adults.

And finally to my S&B girls – Alison Marquardt, Kate McCullough, Lindy Lloyd, Liz Read, Margie Mitchell, Sally Fetherstonhaugh, Sarah Larwill, Simone Lambert and Simonette Varrenti – this book is dedicated to you, because, well, basically, you're all awesome. xxx

About the author

Gabrielle Williams lives in Melbourne and has three kids, one husband and a dog. In the name of research, she has spent time underground with a clandestine group called the Cave Clan, conducted a series of in-depth interviews with a group of notorious art thieves, and spent some time animating strawberries and trawling Tinder. She is the author of the critically acclaimed YA novels *Beatle Meets Destiny*, *The Reluctant Hallelujah* and *The Guy, The Girl, The Artist and His Ex*, all of which have been shortlisted for a number of prestigious awards.